LOVELORN, LOVESTRUCK AND LOVE AT FIRST SIGHT

Also by Alexandria Blaelock

FICTION
That Love Nonsense

MS BLAELOCK'S BOOKS
Stress Free Dinner Parties
Signature Wardrobe Planning
Holistic Personal Finance
Minimally Viable Housekeeping

SHORT STORY COLLECTIONS
The Haunting of Hayward Hall

SHORT STORIES
Alma's Grace
Balancing the Book
Bygone Boyfriend
Carmelita Basingstoke
Fate in Your Hands
Kiss of Death
Lady of the Looking Glass
Life in the Security Directorate
Long Weekend in the Snow
Love in the Security Directorate
Morning Star, Evening Star, Superstar
Needy Bitch
Payton's Run
Phoenix Child
Secret Singer
Shining Star
Ship in a Bottle
Simone Says Hands in the Air
The Day the Schedule Broke
The Guardian's Vigil

LOVELORN, LOVESTRUCK AND LOVE AT FIRST SIGHT

ALEXANDRIA BLAELOCK

Bluemere Books
MELBOURNE, AUSTRALIA

For permission requests, please contact enquiries@bluemerebooks.com.

Ordering Information:
Discounts are available on quantity purchases. For details, contact orders@bluemerebooks.com.

Lovelorn, Lovestruck, and Love at First Sight/Alexandria Blaelock
hardback ISBN: 978-1-925749-47-2
paperback ISBN: 978-1-925749-48-9
digital ISBN: 978-1-925749-49-6

Book Layout © BookDesignTemplates.com

Contents

INTRODUCTION

I love a good romance story, and seeing as you're here, I'm assuming you do too.

What I like best, is being able to try on a new life without having to go to the trouble of getting a divorce and finding a new man.

I can live vicariously through the heroine, without worrying about who's turn it is to wash the dishes, or do the laundry, or take care of the dog deposits.

Fancy being a high-powered New York lawyer whose car breaks down and meets the cutest country bumpkin who arrives to tows her car back to town?

Or a London chef who lives in an athlete's super bachelor pad so she can cook nutritional meals to help him perform at his best, and helps herself to him at the same time?

Or a Melbourne socialite who meets her match in the construction tycoon who wants to tear down the property she's marked for social housing?

It's all good – you don't need to go back to University, lose a bunch of weight or a decade or two.

You can just enjoy your heroine's struggle against herself before she sinks into love. Or lust.

And reminisce about the days you used to wear clothes that were too tight, and didn't need to dye your hair.

And the darker and more miserable it is out there in the real world, the more I want to curl up with something I know where it's going, even if I don't know how it's going to get there.

There's nothing better than a romance when your boss had words with you, your train was delayed, or you had an uncomfortable day at the hospital.

Romance is pretty much the perfect read whenever you've had a shitty day.

Or have to spend a lot of time waiting for appointments, and can't be dealing with long or complicated plots.

With romance, you know the couple will end up together, but not knowing how they'll get there is always exciting.

There is nothing quite as satisfying as closing the book on a happy ending, wiping the tears from your eyes, and getting back to the laundry.

So, here are five of my favourite short romances, (that I've written):

- Cosima meets Fabian, the wannabe Opera Singer on her working holiday.
- Jennifer has business back in her home town, but the only business she's interested in is Jason, the one who got away.
- Sandra works as a scheduler in a movie studio, and Dan, the CEO hopes she'll schedule time for him.
- Christy's a photographer who has a crush on her subject, while Hunter will do just about anything to meet his idol.
- Jessica's a writer, and Jason, the actor hired to play her main character, looks exactly as she imagined him.

So, I'll leave you in their capable hands.

Alexandria Blaelock
Melbourne, Australia
April, 2021

ALEXANDRIA BLAELOCK

AUTHOR OF FATE IN YOUR HANDS

SECRET SINGER

A SHORT STORY

SECRET SINGER

Cosima avoided the old clanky lift and skipped down the long circling flight of stairs instead.

It had to be said that the elegantly imposing stairwell was one of two reasons she'd booked into the hotel in the first place.

The stairs climbed from the ground floor, round and around in marble circles to the fifth floor.

And unlike other old and once-imposing family homes converted into small boutique hotels, this one maintained the same high-quality finishes from the ground to the roof.

No slumming servants in this once prosperous household.

At least not in the main house.

As you descended the stairs (or ascended if you were that way inclined) the light from the glass light well dimmed and brightened as clouds obscured the sun.

Now and again, the light cast the silhouette of a bird against the white plastered wall. Seeming to fly by your side, keeping you company on your long journey to wherever.

Happily, being old stairs, the engineering ensured the smell of cooking stayed beneath them. Only fresh or at least freshly air-conditioned air was sucked upwards.

With a slight hint of some kind of perfuming agent, probably the large fiery bright floral arrangement placed in the centre of a table in the centre of the open ground floor space beneath them.

And as you walked down (or up), leaning over the balustrade, the arrangement provided an incredible, if somewhat dizzying, kaleidoscopic view.

The thick, deep purple plush stair runner was stunning in its plain simplicity, secured against the stair treads with slightly tarnished chrome rods.

It went some way towards containing the echoes, but without other distractions, you could still hear the whispers of other guests waiting for the lifts.

Must have been a fun place for a bit of espionage activity in the house's heyday.

It was also the perfect place to indulge all kinds of fantasies involving tiaras, masked balls, and holiday romances.

Though circular stairs are notoriously difficult to vacuum, and the carpet was in need of a good going over.

From an artistic point of view, Cosima appreciated the variety of refuse that decorated the stairway. Including sparkling paper-lined aluminium foil chewing gum wrappers, glistening pieces of thick, clear cellophane from some kind of packaged snack, and when the sun hit it, a glowing gold coin.

Though the coin was not from a country where she was likely to spend it.

While it is perfectly possible to imagine staid middle-aged astrophysicists, molecular biologists and chemical whatsists named Cosima, our Cosima was almost exactly what you would think to look for if someone said, "hey look; there's Cosima!"

A tiny, dark-haired, imp-faced pixie. Except, perhaps, a little more plumptious, probably due to too much time spent dreaming.

Because, of course, she worked in the creative arts, and spent entirely too much time in her imagination.

As you would.

The second reason she was staying in this particular hotel was the glorious, as well as enormous mural painted in the ground floor Salon.

That the family who owned the hotel hosted free drinks for guests on a Friday night in that very Salon was an added bonus!

However.

Cosima was not actually on vacation, though she would not decline a holiday romance should one be offered.

She was, in fact, part of a gallery exchange pro-gramme - a couple of weeks doing someone else's job in Rome, while that person did hers back home in Australia.

Working holiday!

Best of both worlds.

Having arrived the day before, Cosima was headed downstairs for a spot of breakfast before heading off to her first day of work.

So very exciting.

She might be a bit jet-lagged and close to worn out, but nonetheless, it was all a big adventure.

And she happily imagined hours spent restoring artwork, and designing publicity flyers, and maybe guiding small groups of English-speaking visitors around the gallery.

Half the fun was not knowing what might happen.

And, of course, she also happily imagined the placement as a moody Fellini film, *La Dolce Vita* for example.

Which was why she'd packed a number of slim black dresses for her travel wardrobe. And suitably flat shoes for walking.

Because you just never knew what might come your way.

Breakfast was a wonderfully continental selection of bread, and cheese, and thinly sliced meats, with deliciously sweet, milky coffee.

But by the time she realised there was a selection of cakes and pastries through a side door, it was too late. She was already full of fresh, tasty mozzarella, lightly seasoned and drizzled with olive oil.

It was a short walk to her place of work, or it would have been if she hadn't boldly strode out in entirely the wrong direction and had to take a hair-raising cab ride to get there in time.

No problem. First full day in a big city on the other side of the planet.

That wasn't overflowing with native English speakers.

And sadly, her first day of work was not exactly the Roman holiday she'd been hoping for either. There was some sweeping up after the unboxing of new art, which she was not permitted to touch and barely to look at.

There was some stuffing and stamping of envelopes of promotional materials.

And some fetching and carrying for her new boss and colleagues.

Though it might have been easier had she learned a bit more Italian before she left home.

Despite being told by Vincenzo to throw herself into hamming up the accent, it wasn't quite enough to communicate effectively.

And she felt like a condescending idiot when she did.

The plate of fresh seafood pasta in a light tomato sauce she ate at a sidewalk cafe on the walk back to her hotel helped her mood a great deal.

As did the first and second cold, crisp glasses of Pinot Grigio she drank with it.

Relaxing a little to the recorded background of some kind of opera. Something vaguely familiar. Familiar enough to hum along with, perhaps *Così Fan Tutte*.

Thinking perhaps a show at the *Teatro dell'Opera di Roma* might not go amiss. A cheap seat at a matinee.

Because it was Rome, after all. And she could no more skip the opera than the Trevi Fountain, the *Colleseum*, or the *Piazza di Spagna*.

She greeted Domenico at reception on her way back in, slipped through to the bar and ordered a lovely bitter Campari.

Then took it into a little nook under the stairs to drink while she used the guest computer to check her email.

Which was a lot cheaper (free) than using her phone data (nowhere near free) for the same job.

And seeing as she was there, a couple of searches to confirm the opera at the cafe was *Così Fan Tutte*. She plugged her earbuds into the machine and listed for a while as she sipped her drink.

And as you always do, slipped down a net-rabbit hole and listened to more and more opera. A bit more Mozart, a bit of Puccini, and some Bizet.

She finished her drink, though not her emails, and the tiniest bit drunk, decided it was time for bed anyway.

Naturally, living in her imagination, she took the stairs.

Which turned out to have the perfect rise for a slow, steady and more importantly, elegant upward glide.

Most likely even in a long skirt with an extortion-ate sweep.

Halfway up, she heard a man singing.

In a mesmerising voice - the light, sweet freshness of a tenor, combined with the depth and drama of a baritone.

Like a slightly bitter, dark chocolate brownie.

He took her breath away.

For the duration of the song, she was spellbound.

Hand on the balustrade, one foot on one step, the other on the step above.

Eyes closed, swaying slightly in line with his dramatic interpretation.

Cosima couldn't help wondering why he was hanging out in the hotel and not singing on a stage somewhere.

But of course, competition for places in opera companies must be intense.

Because surely, everyone in Italy must sing opera.

After a moment, she realised he'd stopped singing.

As the echoes dissipated, she heard a slight scuff that suggested he was about to leave.

"Wait!" she cried.

The noise ceased, and she thought perhaps he was indeed waiting.

"Who are you?"

He chuckled, "I am no one *Signorina*," he said in perfect, but lightly accented English.

As of course, he would if he worked in the hotel.

"You sing beautifully."

After a short pause, he said, "*grazie*," and with the slightest whoosh was gone.

Cosima remained where she was, unable for a moment to free herself from his spell.

Even his speaking voice resonated in her rib cage!

If he asked her nicely, she'd walk through hell for him without hesitation.

In fact, he didn't need to ask nicely, she'd probably do it anyway.

Even though she had no idea who he was or what he looked like.

A man of mystery - her Secret Singer - what's not to like?

She challenged herself to figure out who he was, even if it was the only thing she achieved before she went home.

《《 • 》》

Fabian smiled as he returned to the reception desk.

He knew who Cosima was because she'd charmed Domenico so thoroughly, he'd mentioned her several times during handover.

Domenico thought she was so sweet he wanted to swap his own, less sweet adult daughter for her.

But Fabian hadn't realised she'd taken the stairs instead of the lift when he started singing.

And once he'd realised, he felt obliged to finish the song and retreat until later.

His audition wasn't far off now, and he wanted to focus his rehearsal energy on the passages that didn't come easily to him.

In private.

If you could call the foyer of an international hotel at midnight private.

But Domenico was right, she was sweet and charming.

He cheated and looked her up in the booking system.

Here for a little over a week more.

He called up a copy of her passport page and was pleasantly surprised.

She was cute too.

And when he thought about it, he recalled seeing her at breakfast as he ate before leaving work. When he'd been busy flirting with Gabriella.

He hummed a few scales as he shuffled papers around, trying to look busy.

And after a while, he thought it might be fun to play with her a little bit.

If she was game.

And he reckoned, that if she was there the next night, then she was game.

«« • »»

The next day, after a selection of cakes for breakfast, Cosima greeted Domenico on her way out.

She managed to find her way to work, on foot, without getting lost.

Arriving with coffee, her new colleagues greeted her like a long-lost friend.

She enjoyed putting together a small promotional flyer.

It was a great day!

On her way back to the hotel, she stopped at a cafe with a view over the *Colleseum*. Savouring a plate of antipasto on the pavement, with a light, dry Lambrusco, she let the swirl of tourist conversation roll over her.

Ordinary people may have felt lonely at a table for one within a multitude. Astrophysicist Cosima may have buried her face in an academic journal and pretended she didn't mind eating alone.

But our Cosima lived in her imagination.

And at that moment, she was happy to be alone, watching the sky darken.

Because her imagination was trying to put a face on her Secret Singer.

Her location and the fluency of his singing language suggested Italian.

Though his spoken English suggested he either was or had learned from an American.

She hoped he was tall, dark and handsome.

Preferably around her age, slim and well built.

Not older, fatter, uglier.

She was fairly sure he was a hotel employee, not one of the guests, and definitely not Domenico with his raspy smoker's voice.

The singer was sufficiently at ease in his surroundings to sing out loud, taking full advantage of the acoustic conditions. It didn't seem likely a guest would sing so confidently in a strange place.

Or have such a strong operatic presentation.

Plus, he was sober, no slurring his words or losing his diaphragmatic control.

She'd heard him late at night, suggesting night staff.

From the ground floor, so perhaps reception, porter, waiter, bartender.

And at that point, imagination failed her.

She had no idea which of those jobs might make a more attractive man.

Or which might produce the better singer.

Would a porter have the largest lung capacity?

Would a waiter have better voice control?

Someone at reception would be there for the duration of their shift. If any lifting and carrying needed to be done, he'd call someone else to do it, so plenty of time to sing.

And if he was the night receptionist, he would probably only sing if he thought he was alone.

Had he waited for her to leave before singing?

Had he chosen something to sing to her in particular?

Goosebumps rose on her arms, and not just because of the cool breeze rising up the hill.

Anyway, all that kind of ruled out hanging around spying on the ground floor.

The best approach was probably to sit halfway up the stairs and wait for something to happen.

For some reason, she was very glad she'd eliminated the possibility he was a guest.

More romantic that way perhaps.

Less likely to end tragically? Or perhaps more.

A story worthy of its own operatic score.

Passing through reception, she stopped to chat to Domenico, casually discovering he was about to clock off and wishing him a good night.

And getting herself a start time in the region of 8 pm.

Nicely done, she congratulated herself, walking through to the bar.

She climbed onto a barstool and asked for a *digestivo* recommendation.

The cute Australian boy poured her a Caffo Vecchio Amaro del Capo, and they chatted for a short while about places he thought she should visit, and things she should do.

No way he was her Secret Singer mate.

She took her Amaro through to check her email, surreptitiously looking for a man who might be the singer. Though of course, the hotel staff were very discreet and invisible.

Much as she wanted to, she couldn't let herself go through to look in on reception, because that would be cheating.

Nor could she stay up any later, because it had been a long day, and she was knackered.

Besides, if yesterday was anything to go by, he wouldn't start singing until she was out of view.

In the meantime, she rummaged about in her bag for her notebook and lucky hello kitty pen. She tore a page from the book, and scrawled a note, assuming that if he spoke English, he probably could read it and maybe write it too.

Do you take requests?

C

x

She left the note on the computer keyboard and walked up the stairs again.

Slowly, watching the floor, keeping an eye on the keyboard for as long as she was able.

Which wasn't long.

And once again, when she was halfway up, he started singing from the shadows.

Unlike the night before, the tune was familiar, though she didn't know the words. Though that didn't stop her quietly humming along.

And dancing a little, up and down a couple of steps.

Pretending she was wearing a dress with a much longer and wider skirt. Wondering if there was a shop somewhere she could buy something like she was imagining.

It was wonderful.

And all too soon, the song came to an end.

She clapped and called, "*bràvo.*"

"*Grazie.*"

"*Encore.*"

He snorted.

But a moment later, he started singing *That's Amore* in English. And when he reached the chorus, she sang along.

But what she lacked for in skill, she made up in enthusiasm.

And the stairway acoustics didn't hurt either.

"*Magnifica,*" he said as the echoes dissipated.

She laughed, "you flatter me."

"Never."

"Thank you," she said, "I must go now".

"*Buona Notte.*"

"You too," she said and ran up the stairs.

«« • »»

Fabian had been waiting for her to head upstairs.

In fact, he'd been waiting for her all day.

Every time he dozed off for a minute, she'd visited him in his dreams.

Bringing him a small glass of wine.

Pouring some pasta onto a plate.

Rubbing his feet after a hard day at work.

Kissing his head as she bustled about doing some chore or another.

Looking after their children.

Standing beside him at some red-carpet event or another.

Not bad for someone he'd never met.

He'd risked sneaking out to see the note she'd left, and wondered what kind of request she might have to make.

And due to the cant of the stairs, he'd been able to watch her dancing, knowing she thought she was unobserved.

And oh my God, she was adorable.

Could not sing to save her life

But twelve out of ten for enthusiasm.

Too adorable.

Like a puppy, only with better manners.

He grinned and pulled the cuffs of his shirt down as he returned to reception.

Looked like she wanted to play.

So what should his next move be?"

«« • »»

Cosima skipped down the stairs.

Partly because "hey it's Roma!" and partly because she was eager to see if her Secret Singer had answered her note.

It was where she'd left it, wedged between the keys of the computer keyboard, and for a moment, she was disappointed.

Had he not seen her note?

Had he not answered?

She took a quick look around, and finding she was alone, tiptoed over the marble floor to pick it up.

At a glance, she could see an extra line of writing, in a strong, firm hand, and folded the paper into her pocket to look at later.

She assembled a breakfast of *Bresaola* with *Caprese* salad and picked at it while she thought about his reply.

Kiss me if you can find me.

Very forward for someone she hadn't met.

Yet the idea of kissing the man she imagined was incredibly exciting.

Lord help them both if he was short and fat and ugly.

But he *sounded* young!

And confident.

And gorgeous.

And even if he was short and fat and ugly, she was out of there before too long anyway.

Even if he was tall and thin and beautiful, she was out of there.

But if he was...

Well?

Challenge accepted.

Her workday was varied and interesting, but her thoughts were with her Secret Singer.

He'd upped the stakes, so did that mean she could hang around the ground floor eavesdropping on all the male staff members?

Or would it be better to stick to her own self-imposed rules?

Or just enjoy the flirtation while it lasted, and go home with a great holiday story?

Though, stories need endings.

If she told anyone about him, they'd want to know who he was, and whether he was a good kisser.

And did they go any further, and was she going back to see him, or was he coming to her.

She could make up some nonsense, but they would that wasn't how the story was supposed to end.

Cosima was assuming he wanted her to find him.

And that he knew who she was.

But did he?

Would he reveal himself if she didn't unmask him before she left?

Would he say, "such a shame *Signorina*, we could've had so much fun. Never mind, have a good trip home, and a long and happy life".

Or was he just winding her up?

A bit of fun with the tourist to laugh about later with his friends.

But how could a man with an opera hero's voice be the villain in real life?

Driven by curiosity, she stopped at the Chinese restaurant next to the hotel for some food on her way back. And happily, she could get a simple plate of mixed dumplings to go with her rice wine.

How surprising that while they were definitely what she ordered, they were a little more Italian in flavour and style than the ones she was used to back home.

She was enjoying the last of the rice wine when she realised that she'd started listening to a conversation going on behind her.

It wasn't the words, because she didn't speak enough Italian to understand them, but there was something, aside from a Chinese accent that had snagged her attention.

Like an itch, she couldn't reach to scratch.

She looked over her shoulder and noticed a man in the dark hotel uniform at the payment counter. He had thick, dark hair, broad shoulders and slim hips.

And then her attention was stolen by the aroma of chilled coconut pudding, and she smiled at the waiter bringing it to her.

It looked delicious. She closed her eyes and savoured the flavour as she let the first semi-sweet morsel dissolve in her mouth.

And flicked them open again as she realised why the conversation had infiltrated her consciousness - the man at the counter was speaking with the Secret Singer's voice.

She'd seen the Secret Singer!

She dropped the spoon and swung around, but he was out of her view, and there was no one at the register.

He might be gone, but now she knew what the back of him looked like.

And as a dark suit wearer, he couldn't be a red-jacketed porter. She'd already disqualified the barman, so that left reception and waiters.

She picked up her spoon, and took another taste of her dessert, smiling a little as she luxuriated in the flavour.

Fully appreciating the knowledge that he was at the tall, and thin, and beautiful end of the spectrum.

So what should be her next move?

All she had to do was linger a little linger over dinner, and if he was the night receptionist, she'd see him on her way in.

And that was a very tempting thought, but she was enjoying the chase.

She finished her dessert, paid the bill and left.

Greeting Domenico on her way into the reception.

Following her usual routine, she took a drink to the guest computer. A dark, rich, thick, hot chocolate.

It might not have been the best choice, soon she was yawning, and decided to call it a night.

She unfolded the note they'd been sharing, turned it ninety degrees and added another line.

I nearly caught you today.

C

x

And wedged it once more between the keys of the keyboard.

Then slowly climbed the elegant staircase, but he did not sing before she reached her room.

She leaned over the bannister but didn't see or hear anything to suggest he was nearby.

She yawned again.

Then quietly went to bed.

But first, she made a dinner reservation at the hotel restaurant for the following night.

《《 • 》》

Fabian was distraught.

She wasn't there!

She'd gone, and he'd missed her.

Okay, maybe not distraught. Maybe more like puzzled. Perplexed.

And then he saw the note wedged into the keyboard.

He picked it out and took it back to the reception desk.

He leaned one hip against the counter as he read the note.

Where had she been that she'd seen him without her seeing him?

He'd just picked up a takeout next door...

Ah.

《《 • 》》

Cosima skipped down the stairs, straight across to the guest computer, and removed the note before heading to breakfast.

I'm sorry I missed you

Sorry he didn't see her at the restaurant?

Sorry she didn't talk to him?

Sorry he nearly got caught?

Sorry she didn't catch him?

Sorry about what exactly?

What kind of stupid message was that?

And why was she annoyed about it?

She was leaving soon anyway.

Nothing was going to come of this flirtation.

And she didn't know who he was anyway. Some nicely shaped, dark-haired man with a mesmerising voice.

She reviewed her romantic options back home; Tom from accounts, that guy she kept running into at the gym, Greg whom she'd known for 100 years.

None of them as fascinating as her Secret Singer.

She was in a bit of a mood when she left for work.

And it was the kind of mild wrongness that leached into everything she touched.

She dropped her scalding hot coffee, and not only was she in the splash zone but Signora Cardarelli the gallery executive was too. The prospect of an enormous dry-cleaning bill was not pleasant.

She glued her fingers together, and it was only the application of a strong (and highly irritating) solvent that prevented a trip to hospital to have them separated.

She lost her credit card while buying pain killers, and spent forever on the phone to her bank to cancel it and paying an enormous fee to have a replacement card expressed to the hotel.

She was tired and sore and still grumpy when she got back to the hotel. And not even a long soak in a hot bath was enough to dispel the mood.

Especially as her hand was sore and wrapped in bandages.

Though on the bright side, it was her left hand and she was right-handed.

And she'd made a reservation for dinner, so didn't need to leave the hotel.

Though she was tempted to cancel it and have room service deliver something.

Under different circumstances, she would've enjoyed it. Just a little asparagus risotto with Pinot Grigio, followed by strawberries macerated in Moscato.

And she stayed just long enough to discover her Secret Singer was not a waiter.

The only option left was the night receptionist.

A young man Domenico described as "a bit wild."

Cosima barely knew what to think about that.

Despite preferring the lift, which was taking forever, she forced herself up the stairs.

And when she hit the usual spot, he started singing.

She paused, looked up at the ceiling above her, and then the stairs beneath her.

She was tired, and in pain, and wanted nothing more than to curl up in her own bed, with her own pillows and her dog.

Why, she wondered, was she even playing this stupid game of hide and seek with a stranger?

A stranger who was a bit wild.

Which could mean anything from liked to drink a little too much and recklessly sleep with too many women, to being some kind of mafia enforcer who left horse heads in people's beds.

A game that in such a short time had taken over her life. Rendering her barely able to breathe without thinking about him.

Some crazy guy she'd never met.

She took a deep breath and kept walking.

«« • »»

Fabian wondered if she was all right.

She hadn't left him a note and barely paused on her way up the stairs.

Hadn't acknowledged him in the slightest.

He was offended.

Well, maybe not offended, more like disappointed.

She was the only person who'd commented on his night time singing.

And at a loss to explain her lack of interest in continuing their game.

Aside from whatever injury her bandaged hand represented.

About the only option left to him for contact was the Friday night soiree.

Assuming she attended.

Unless...

«« • »»

Cosima was writing in her journal when the doorbell chimed, and she opened the door before she remembered it was a good idea to ask who was there first.

A porter held a small tray containing a glass of some kind of liqueur, a slice of dark cake, and a small, sealed packet of painkillers.

"I didn't order this," she said.

"Nonetheless, it's marked for delivery to this room."

"From who?"

"I don't know, but I expect the sender thought you would."

"I see. Well, thank you."

The porter emptied the tray onto the desk while she signed the chit, then left.

Cosima surveyed the delivery with suspicion and noticed a folded paper. She opened it and recognised the handwriting.

Feel better soon

One the one hand, a lovely surprise.

On the other, her Secret Singer definitely knew who she was.

And which room she was in.

Something else that suggested reception.

And a gift that firmed up a more positive interpretation of what "sorry I missed you" might mean.

Mmmmm! Frangelico and chocolate cake.

It was a much happier Cosima who went to bed.

«« • »»

Fabian watched her eat cake for breakfast, smiling slightly at the evident relish with which she ate.

Clearly feeling better this morning than the night before.

And tonight was the soiree...

«« • »»

Cosima enjoyed a much better day at work.

Her colleagues were sympathetic, Signora Cardarelli brushed aside her offers to pay for the cleaning, and the *Farmacia* called to say they'd found her card.

Not that it mattered; she'd already cancelled it, but it was still an amazing stroke of luck.

And she knew tonight was the night her Secret Singer would be revealed.

Though what would happen next was something she didn't even want to imagine.

Because no matter what it was, she was still leaving in a few days.

If the outcome was positive, she'd room to manoeuvre on her visa, and vacation days owing to her.

Though should she extend her visit, and should they spend more time together, it would just make leaving that much harder.

Not quite the sword of Damocles, but a bitter-sweet situation.

Cosima reminded herself not to get ahead of her-self.

He might not even be there.

That did not prevent her buying a new dress on her way back to the hotel.

Nor did it stop her getting her hair washed, trimmed and styled.

Or getting a manicure, or buying a new lipstick.

She paid particular attention to her grooming - shaving her legs, applying her makeup more carefully than normal, and adding a spritz of duty-free perfume.

And paced up and down the landing so as not to be the first one arriving at the Salon.

As she walked slowly down the stairs, the long, full skirt of her new, floral silk dress caressed her clean-shaven legs. The sharp ends of her fresh cut hair scratched her shoulders.

Nearing the bottom, she could hear the slight murmur of conversation and clink of glasses, and smell something rich and savoury.

As she entered the Salon, she accepted a glass of a rich and complex flavoured Aglianico from the Australian barman, nodding her thanks as she took her first sip.

She heard a conversation in English and headed over to join the table, listening to the discussion of sites to see, and things to do. Making mental notes on what to follow up.

And as her glass lowered, she watched the waiters circulate the room, trying to pick her Secret Singer. But they were too tall, or short, or thin, or fat.

She was beginning to feel like Goldilocks.

Until his voice came from behind her, "*Signorina?*"

She paused for a moment, and closed her eyes, nervous about what she might see.

And then she opened them and turned to meet his green eyes.

He was beautiful.

Square jaw, clean-shaven, slight smile.

Smelling citrusy clean and fresh.

He topped up her glass, then moved to top up the others at the table, and onto the next table.

They were limited by the fact of his being at work.

So Cosima contented herself by moving her chair slightly to watch him.

He circulated the room, chatted with guests, waited at the bar, talked with his colleagues.

Now and again, he looked at her and smiled slightly.

She couldn't help but smile back, as she imagined marriage, children, grandchildren with him.

An entire lifetime, even though they hadn't really spoken, and didn't know each other.

She watched him make another round, allowed him to top up her glass.

And watched the guests start to leave.

She watched him collect used glasses, join the other waiters in tidying the room, and disappear through a door with the empties.

And then she sat alone with what was left of her drink.

Wondering what came next.

«« • »»

Fabian watched her.

She was so still, she could almost be a statue.

He'd made arrangements to take the night off, so he could take her to a club or something. But she looked so elegant, self-contained and unattainable, he was afraid to ask.

Then again, she seemed to be waiting for him.

And if he didn't ask, he'd never know.

He loosened his tie.

She sighed.

Then drained her glass, stood up, and glanced around the room.

Was she looking for him?

Whatever.

He pushed himself through the door before he could change his mind.

She turned and looked at him.

And smiled.

He smiled and walked towards her, "would you care to go out for something to eat?"

«« • »»

Cosima smiled.

It had been an amazing trip.

She'd extended her stay, Fabian had taken some time off work, and he'd taken her to see some extraordinary sites. The ones she'd hoped to see, but hadn't expected to; Pompeii, Capri, the Amalfi Coast, and Tuscany.

They'd eaten delicious food, drunk fine wines, and tumbled into bed together.

But the spark just wasn't there.

It was such a shame.

He hugged her and kissed her forehead as he let her go, "when you come back, give me a call."

"I will," though they both knew it wasn't likely.

"And when you come to Australia, look me up."

"I will," though they both knew that was even less likely.

"I'm sorry—" he said, and at the same time she said, "it's a shame—"

And they both laughed.

"Why don't we meet up in a decade?" Fabian asked.

"Where do you suggest?"

"Somewhere neither of us have been."

They rattled through countries and cities, and Cosima suggested Tokyo.

Fabian did a quick internet search on his phone and suggested a hotel.

They agreed a date and added it to the calendars in their phones.

"Marry me if *you* don't find anyone else in the meantime," he said.

She made a non-committal noise, "marry me if you don't find anyone else in the meantime."

They laughed again.

"I'll hold you to it," he said.

"I hope so."

She turned and walked towards the departure lounge, looking back at him and waving before walking through the doors.

An amazing trip that had her questioning whether there needed to be a spark.

Or whether you could build a satisfying relationship on friendship.

«« • »»

Fabian watched her leave and felt the light of the day dim around him.

He'd miss her.

His phone cheeped, and he took it out to read the text

miss you already

He wondered what the Visa situation was in Australia.

miss you more

he replied.

THE END

ALEXANDRIA BLAELOCK

AUTHOR OF FATE IN YOUR HANDS

THE BYGONE BOYFRIEND

A SHORT STORY

THE BYGONE BOYFRIEND

Jennifer strolled down Perth's main street.

When she was younger, the City had seemed so big and so busy.

But having lived in cities ten or more times the size, across Europe, Asia and America, now it just seemed quaint.

So small and slow it barely moved at all.

A cute holiday town - great to visit, but not to live.

Like a beach holiday, without the beach.

Or getting off the train while it was still moving.

She struggled to summon up a feeling of attachment to the city she'd grown up in.

The one most would define as her home town, even though she'd chosen not to return.

Hadn't intended ever to come back.

The late afternoon sunshine was warm against her back, too warm in fact, though that was to be expected given it was Summer.

The golden Summer sun was about the only thing that felt the same as she remembered. Though it rarely rains when you remember your childhood does it?

The city's sights, sounds and smells were all wrong, it wasn't like home at all.

The ghosts of past friends, jobs, and dates swirling around her didn't help at all.

The café where she'd bought her first cappuccino was now a cut-price makeup outlet.

The movie theatre where she'd fallen in love with Monty Python while watching *Life of Brian* was a lap dancing club.

Not even her old office building had escaped unscathed.

It was now a discounted hotel, and she'd come within a hair's breadth of trying to book a room where her desk used to be.

Only the corporate travel policy and prospects for reimbursement prevented it.

The travel agent she'd bought her one-way ticket out of this hell hole was a lingerie shop. Selling a better class of lingerie than had been available before she'd left.

And possibly worst of all, her Friday night drinking hole, where you could spin the wheel and win a hot roasted chicken for a late-night drunken snack, was now an underground car park.

Tired of walking, she stopped at an open-air bar in the mall.

When she'd left, it had been a four-lane street jam-packed with traffic, two traffic lights away from the train station. Now it was an open space on top of a recently constructed underground station.

She pushed her way through the tourists, and took a seat at a table, resting her bag on the seat next to her.

Large trees grew from holes in the paving. They weren't particularly tall yet, only just reaching the second story of the surrounding buildings, but they shaded the pedestrians milling beneath them well enough.

She admired the way the City had invested in re-development in line with the vision of a prosperous and popular international city.

If you build it, and all that, though they still had a way to go.

Or was she witnessing the pivot between thriving metropolis and ghost town?

A slight exhaust scented breeze fanned the leaves and cooled her face.

She leaned back in her seat and hooked a foot around the seat opposite to pull it closer.

Then kicked off her sandals, put her bare feet on the chair, and her hands behind the back of her neck.

The breeze blew through the loose weave of her shirt, evaporating the sweat from her body.

The place couldn't have been more alien if it was a city she'd never visited before.

Though technically, this City wasn't the one she'd left, but the one that had replaced it.

She'd only been away for 15 years, but she had an idea of how Rip Van Winkle might have felt when he woke up.

Everything was the same, only different. Where there'd once been a feeling of love, there was now re-vulsion.

It felt like the City was judging her, and unlike her dog, it didn't forgive her long absence.

Though time must move differently for dogs than Cities.

When a waitress in a long black apron arrived, she ordered Campari and soda, and a bowl of marinated olives.

Despite the City's rejection, it was sort of nice to be alone, unknown and unnoticed in the crowd.

To have some quiet space away from her worries, both here and at home.

She sighed, and stretched, pushing her toes toward the back of the chair, and opening her arms further behind her neck.

Then she took her black straw hat off, put it on top of her bag and ruffled her hair.

The stiffening breeze was pleasant against her sweaty scalp.

Her bag pinged, and she pulled her phone out to see what her assistant wanted.

No changes to the presentation, good luck tomorrow, make time to have some fun.

Excellent news; time contingency not required, and she had the night off.

Her drink arrived, and she drank half of it before the ice could melt and water it down. Then went back to watching the people.

Even though she knew it was unlikely she'd see anyone familiar, she couldn't help looking for familiar faces in the steady stream of people leaving the City as quickly as possible.

She wondered what her old friends might be like. Would they reject her as completely as the City had? Had she grown beyond them too?

She closed her eyes and tried to imagine what calling her one-time best friend might be like.

Though she'd have to make a few phone calls to get Amy's number.

Might be a bit of a conversation required to get it too, Amy's mother had never liked her much.

Come to think of it, most of her friend's mothers hadn't liked her much either.

Was that because of something she'd done, or because her Dad was the town drunk?

She'd never know for sure, though it stood to reason they thought she was a "bad" girl and a "bad" influence. Still not entirely sure what that was.

She hadn't given it much thought at the time, aside from thinking it was funny.

Anyway, there was really only Jason she wouldn't mind seeing again.

Though the prospect was terrifying.

She'd loved him to the peak of embarrassing obsession, and treated him so badly at the end.

Then again, he'd cheated on her with Helen back then, so wasn't her fury justified?

Though in retrospect, she appreciated his bluntness. He'd given her what she'd needed to make a clean break, move away and forge a new life for herself.

Ridiculously, of all the things she'd done and not done, she regretted not sleeping with him the most.

And if she stumbled across a time machine, she'd be tempted to haul the chrononaut out and take a trip back to fix that.

She snorted at the idea.

Poor innocent Jason wouldn't know what hit him - some old to him woman cracking on to him and not taking the hint when he politely asked her to leave him alone.

Just as well you can't go back, only go forward. Some things are better left in the past where they belong.

And this time tomorrow, she'd be on her way back home to her normal life, leaving Jason and this town behind her, in the past where they belonged.

But what was she afraid of?

That the town knew who she really was, and wasn't fooled by the veneer of confidence she showed to the world?

That it saw her for the damaged little girl she had been, not the competent woman she'd become.

And as for Jason, did she think after all this time she'd lose control of herself and beg him to take her back?

Or was she more afraid she'd not be able to resist him should he call her back?

One thing for sure, there were way too many memories in this town, and the sooner she left them behind, the better.

If they won the bid, someone else could take over the negotiations.

«« • »»

Jason wouldn't have noticed her if she hadn't suddenly leant over to check her phone as he was walking along the balcony above her.

And even then, he might not have noticed her at all if she hadn't seemed so brisk, efficient and stunningly well-groomed in comparison to the drooping, ill-dressed tourists sitting in Garibaldi's Bar.

Located just about where exhaustion hit, Garibaldi's was a bit of a tourist trap. And as usual, it was full of grubby limp t-shirts.

Except for the woman in the crisp white linen shirt, and black straw hat.

There was something about her that pulled at the edge of his memory like a hangnail.

Despite himself, he paused, leaning on the balustrade to watch her, trying to figure it out so he could forget about her and focus on to his blind date.

She took her hat off, tilting her head back to reveal dark red coloured lips and ruffling her short hair with matching red nail polish tipped fingers.

There was an economy about her movements, an angular fluidity as if she was the living embodiment of the linen she was wearing.

She took up space, looking like the kind of independent woman who's more accustomed to giving orders than taking them.

It was a little bit sexy.

Then he caught a glimpse of her face between the leaves and realised who she was.

Jennifer Hughes.

His first love, Jennifer Hughes.

The girl he'd foolishly dumped for another, who'd dumped him not long after.

Jennifer, who wasn't wearing any rings!

He'd hurt her feelings so deeply he was ashamed to go back to her and ask her forgivingness.

She'd moved away, and so far as he knew, had never been back.

Blind date forgotten, he turned and headed back towards the stairs. He had to get down there and make contact before he lost her again.

He walked up and down beside the bar a few times, hoping she'd see him and call out to him, or maybe leave so he could run into her.

No such luck.

Maybe she didn't recognise him.

He walked towards a shop window and assessed his reflection, then smoothed back his hair.

A girl inside started laughing, and he quickly turned away, assuming she was laughing at him.

Then, pausing to take a deep breath, he plunged into the bar before he could change his mind.

«« • »»

"Jennifer?" a male voice asked.

The sound of her name startled her, but she didn't believe he was talking to her, so she didn't open her eyes and tried to ignore the voice.

Clearly, it was some other Jennifer.

"Jennifer Hughes, is that you?"

No doubting it now, he was talking to her.

She opened her eyes and looked up into a vaguely familiar face.

"It's me, Jason Spencer."

She looked more closely, and yes; it probably was him.

What was it Mum used to say, think of the devil and he's sure to appear?

Looks like she was right about that after all.

Jennifer hoped the wind didn't change then, the look on her face was probably not the most attractive in her arsenal.

Campari on an empty stomach got in her way as she struggled to get her feet back on the ground and sit upright.

He was older, naturally, more relaxed in his body and confident about himself.

His snug t-shirt and well-fitted jeans didn't hide the fact his weedy body had filled out with muscle, the kind of muscle that hinted at hard work rather than hours in the gym.

His blazer suggested he was headed to a date, and she felt a flash of jealousy.

Jason Spencer wasn't a boy any more, he'd become a man and a fine-looking man at that.

"Ah, hello, Jason. Long-time no see," and she winced.

Oh God, had she really said those stupid words?

He smiled, and sat down uninvited, "you look just the same."

"God I hope not. I hope I look like I know what I'm doing now."

He laughed, his one-time wind chime giggle, now deepened to a chuckle.

He gestured to attract the waitress' attention, "Heineken please," and pointing at her glass, "and another of those."

The waitress smiled and nodded, much friendlier towards him than Jennifer.

"Well, looks like you've still got it," she said, slightly miffed.

He snorted, "Not as much as you might think, I'm old and irrelevant now."

"I think I might know that feeling better than you."

He snorted again.

"How's Helen?" Jennifer asked, needing to get that out of the way first.

"Who?"

"Helen. You must remember Helen."

"Oh, yeah. Helen. We broke up years ago. I'm surprised you remember her."

Oops, Jennifer thought.

"So, how's it going?" he asked.

She guessed that was code for "are you single," but she was here for one night only.

She wouldn't mind fucking him out of curiosity, but it couldn't be any more than that.

Unless he was very good and then she might stretch to twice before she went home.

Anything more than that was a recipe for disaster.

But as he smiled at her, she had the idea he might be interested in a night or more with her.

"Fine," she took a gulp of her drink, "busy. You?"

She looked at her watch to emphasise how busy she was, but he laughed, and she rested her wrist on the table.

He covered her hand with his, gently stroking the back of her hand with his thumb.

She noticed he wasn't wearing any rings.

Not that it meant much, but, he wasn't wearing any rings.

"I don't think you're busy. And I have an idea you're not fine too."

She went still, watching him smile at her, feeling the exquisite torture of his soft touch.

It felt like he was staking a claim.

Realising she was losing the battle, she tried to pull her hand back, but he tightened his grip slightly, and after a couple of tugs, she let him keep it.

She opened her mouth to deny it, but on a purely objective level, it was the truth.

She wasn't fine or busy.

"How's your mother?" she asked, trying to turn the conversation in a different direction.

"The same. If you have time, I'm sure she'd love to see you."

Jennifer smiled, Mrs Spencer was the only mother she'd known who'd seemed to see her, not her family.

"I wish I could, but I'm leaving tomorrow."

The waitress arrived with their drinks, bumping Jennifer.

Waking her up.

"Thank you," said Jason, releasing her hand and reaching for his drink.

"Thank you," Jennifer said simultaneously, and the waitress smiled and nodded in acknowledgement as Jason shouted, "Jinx! Now you have to grant me a wish."

She grimaced and drained the last of her first drink.

"What's your wish then?"

"Have dinner with me."

Jinx or not, she knew she ought to say no, and took a sip of her fresh drink to stall.

"Say you'll have dinner with me."

One and a bit cocktails with half a bowl of olives aren't the best foundation for rational decision making.

And it would be nice to spend an evening sitting at a table, eating with a person, not cross-legged on the couch eating with the dog.

There would be plenty more of those evenings when she got back home.

She looked at her watch again, and he quirked an eyebrow at her.

Why was she supposed to be avoiding him again?

"I'll have dinner with you."

His face lit up, and he was so dazzling she couldn't change her mind.

Or tell him she only said it because he told her to.

《《 • 》》

She said yes!

Well not technically yes, but at least she didn't say no.

He knew he was grinning like a lunatic, and took a swig of beer to cover it.

Then his phone rang.

Shit! The blind date.

She settled more comfortably into her seat, picked up her drink, and rested it on her lip with an air of resignation he didn't much like.

He couldn't afford to give her any time to change her mind.

So, he pulled his phone from his jacket, turned it off without looking at it, and slipped it back in his pocket.

He grinned again at her surprise.

If she was leaving tomorrow, the stakes were high, and he had to do something to intrigue her. Something to keep her interested and her attention focused on him.

Could he gamify the evening?

"If I dared you, would you turn your phone off too?"

She snorted, "there's no need to dare me, there's no one I'd answer right now."

She pulled her phone from her bag and turned it off.

No one she wanted to talk to!

"It's kind of old fashioned isn't it, not stressing about the phone ringing?"

"Speak for yourself," she said. "My sister and I always raced each other to get to the phone first, though it was more often for her than for me."

"Well, we had walkie-talkies, remember?"

She snorted. "Oh yeah.

"Talking to each other in bed seemed very naughty, didn't it? I was terrified my mother would find out."

He fist-pumped inside, he'd got her thoughts into bed with him, even if they were only 12 at the time.

She softened a little into her chair as if thinking about the age before everything started to get more complicated was relaxing.

Though compared to all the complications of being an adult, maybe it was.

He tilted his beer bottle and started peeling the label off, "those were the days, weren't they?"

"I dunno, so much has happened since then. That girl seems as much a stranger to me as the City does right now."

The ice in her glass clinked, and a drip of condensation fell in her lap.

"Do you sometimes wish you were still a child?" he asked.

"God no. When you're a girl, there's always someone telling you what to do and how to behave."

He laughed.

"Kind of like stop running, or shouting, or tracking dirt through the house?"

"More like pull your skirt down, why don't you smile, why can't you act more like a lady."

"I never noticed."

"How could you? You only had brothers."

They fell silent for a moment while he struggled to understand childhood from a girl's perspective.

"I don't seem to recall you being very ladylike."

"Exactly," she laughed. "Not much has changed since then."

He leaned towards her, "I think I like this version of you. You're sort of more substantial."

"Substantial? I'm not sure that's a compliment."

He leaned his elbows on the table as he leaned closer.

"When you were a kid, you had a knack of disappearing into the background, almost as if you turned sideways and disappeared."

She laughed a little, "you learn to disappear when you live in a house full of drunken violence. That's why I liked your place, it always felt safe."

"I can't even imagine what that must have been like."

She put her drink down and patted his hand, "you're the lucky one then."

He captured her hand as she pulled away and kissed the back of it, "I'm sorry you had to go through that."

"What doesn't kill you makes you stronger hey?

Anyway, those experiences made me who I am to-day. I'm afraid to think who I might have become if things had been any different."

He swallowed his thickening throat. Who would she have become if he hadn't been blinded by Helen?

"I'm starving," she said, "what were you thinking for dinner."

It didn't matter, as long as it wasn't anywhere near where his blind date was waiting. Should it be some-where she hadn't been, or somewhere they'd used to go together?

"Do you remember the food court we used to buy lunch when we came into town to go to the pictures?"

She smiled, "what was it? Golden Palace? Dragon Inn?"

"Doesn't matter, that dive's gone now, but there's an excellent Japanese restaurant there now. Give it a try?"

"Sure," she said, gulping her drink and collecting her bag and hat, "let's go."

《《 • 》》

Jennifer was still lost in a haze of childhood mem-ories. Building dams with Jason, playing hide and seek with Jason, comparing naked boy and girl bits with Jason.

In retrospect, they were lucky no one had found their cubby house. That's one of the benefits of living on the outskirts of a city she supposed.

They'd been so much a part of each other's lives until their late teens. From this great distance, it was amazing she'd let someone else come between them. That she hadn't sent him away to Helen with her best wishes but kept in touch.

Or had that been more to do with Helen?

As they walked, she started thinking about the next day as a different kind of next day.

This thing between them didn't have to be a start, it could be an end instead.

She could take him back to her reasonably priced, reasonably central hotel and do that thing she'd been regretting.

It might have been the Campari talking, but why not get him out of her system, get some psychobabble closure, and go home the next day with no regrets.

So when he took her hand, she laced her fingers through his and told herself it didn't matter that their hands still fit perfectly.

Despite having lived in Tokyo for several years, she let him order the food.

She sat on one hip on her cushion, leaning towards him, legs to the other side.

Maybe a little closer than necessary, but he didn't seem to mind.

It seemed the time for talking was done for the moment, as they focused on the food.

He was right, it was delicious, as well as beautifully prepared and arranged as Japanese food always is.

She placed a little eel on his rice to try, and he put a little chicken on hers. And laughed when he duelled with her chopsticks for a share of the seaweed salad.

He filled her Saki cup, and after taking a sip, she offered it back to him. He held her eyes as he drained the cup, then refilled it and handed it back.

Now and again, she let her hand brush his, or leaned against him.

He nudged her shoulder with his or patted her thigh.

And as the meal came to an end, and he started stacking up the dishes, she was filled with affection for him.

He was the first person she could remember outside of her family.

And now they were sitting together, as comfortably as if they'd never been apart.

All of a sudden, she understood.

Whether they'd been together or not, he'd always been the bedrock of her life.

The only person she'd ever pushed back against, was him.

«« • »»

Jason was focused on stacking the dishes back the way they'd arrived when he realised Jennifer had gone still.

He wasn't afraid exactly, but sensed the change meant something, so he looked at her just as she reached across to kiss him.

Just a little peck, presumably meant for his cheek.

But it was enough for him.

He left the dishes where they were and reached out one hand to cup her jaw, watching for some sign of rejection.

He saw none and slowly leaned towards her to kiss her lips.

So slowly, it seemed she got impatient and leaned towards him, grabbing his face in both hands and kissing his lips.

She'd done the same thing for their first proper kiss, which was just as well because he'd been almost as scared then as he was now.

What if he was doing it wrong, what if she didn't like it, what if she left him.

But this time, she was the one who wanted her independence - how many times had she said she was leaving?

You couldn't fault her for warning him, but it made him wonder.

What was he willing to put on the line to keep her? Could he risk everything the way she had back then?

She broke off the kiss and dropped her hands.

He looked at her for a while, looking for some sign of what she was thinking.

Could he let the dice fall, knowing they were loaded in her favour?

Knowing he was going to lose her, and knowing if he wanted her, he'd have to chase her?

Could he live with himself if he let this opportunity pass?

No.

He couldn't.

"Shall we get out of here?"

《« • »》

Back at her disappointingly unsexy hotel room, Jennifer tried not to let her nerves get in the way.

She wasn't a teenager anymore, and should he care to, Jason could read her life's history mapped in the scars on her body.

Out of defiance, she left the lights on as he peeled back her clothing to reveal her practical underwear and the first of her surgical scars.

He winced but didn't say anything, only kissed each one as he uncovered it.

Perhaps he could see past it, through the girl she had been to the woman she was today.

Not that it mattered, she still couldn't stay.

But she started to wonder whether there was a Jason shaped space in her life.

She'd gone too far from her life here, and she had too much to lose.

She couldn't let it all go to come back to him now.

She shrugged her thoughts away, and for the next few hours, focused on the sensations he roused in her body.

And after a point, fell asleep in his arms.

She woke early the next morning and left him sleeping while she took a shower and dressed.

As she did her makeup, she watched him in the mirror for a while, trying to decide whether he was really asleep or just pretending because he didn't know what to say to her.

But given his masterful performance, there was no need for him to be embarrassed, and he probably deserved his rest.

She quietly packed her carry-on bag and wheeled it to the door. And then she picked his clothes off the floor and folded them on the chair.

It was too late now, but she wished she'd woken him up for another round before she left.

All that was left was to decide whether she wanted to see him again or not.

And she'd probably be less upset to see him again than not, so what to do?

A long time ago he'd cheated on her, and he'd given her a blunt assessment of her future potential with him.

That was, nil.

Though, if the last night had been any indication, he might have changed his mind.

And if he had, then he should pursue her.

If he didn't, then she'd know it was over.

She'd let him choose.

Smiling, she stood at the hotel desk and pulled out some paper and an envelope. She wrote a small note.

Had fun, call if you dare.
 J

She folded the note into the envelope and put it on top of his clothes where he was unlikely to miss it.

It had been fun, and it would be interesting to see what came next.

THE END

ALEXANDRIA BLAELOCK

AUTHOR OF FATE IN YOUR HANDS

THE DAY THE SCHEDULE BROKE

A SHORT STORY

THE DAY THE SCHEDULE BROKE

Sandra (not Sandy, Sands or Sando) pushed a stack of papers aside, then cursed as it over-balanced and slipped off her wonky desk in a cascading flurry of individual sheets across the floor.

She leaned across to her left and looked around her desk at the once organised, colour coded, sticky noted, highlighted and marked-up schedule pages currently strewn haphazardly across the tiny area of worn grey carpet not currently stacked with racks of boxes of props and equipment.

It was the kind of filing crisis that would take twice as long to reorder as it would to reprint. And version control be damned, very tempting to simply sweep it into a corner under the racking and leave it to gather dust like the crushed and torn boxes stored within them.

Her tiny basement office, dimly lit by one small street-level window (and a bare flickering light globe) was literally a storage cupboard before she moved in.

Technically, it still was a storage cupboard, though she wasn't entirely sure whether she was leftover junk in storage or not.

Her pay still landed neatly and on time in her bank account, suggesting not mothballed, but the room's damp, musty smell of forgotten dreams and hopes contended she was in storage.

Or perhaps some kind of black hole event horizon she couldn't escape was a better description.

Frozen in time and place.

She pushed her chair back, and in doing so, knocked the desk off its chock of exactly two and a half pads of sticky notes.

And set in motion a Rube Goldberg style chain re-action of levers and ratchets and spinning wheels and falling things that resulted in a box of light reflectors resettling at precisely the right angle to cast the mess on the floor and dust motes floating in the air in a magical golden glow.

Something clockwork, somewhere in the storage rack started ticking rapidly for a moment, before slowing down, getting slower and slower and finally stopping leaving the room eerily still and silent.

Worse, in some undefinable way than it had been before.

Like her time had run out.

Sandra sighed.

Some days started bad and just got worse.

She started quietly muttering swear words, cursing the day she'd agreed to take up the Project Scheduler contract with Gorgon Studios.

No, not just that.

Maybe as far back as her first job with Con.

Con by name, con by nature.

Was that far enough back? Or should it be the first day she met him?

A chance encounter leading to her first project role, the start of a successful project career, and finally here, now in this pathetic excuse for an office, full of broken-down rubbish, working with a bunch of morons.

Surely that was enough now.

Surely it was time to move on to some other job where she had a habitable place to work and was treated with a little respect.

Was it not?

She made a grab for her bag and jacket hanging on the old fashioned hat stand (also broken), but they were caught up in the hooks, and the whole thing fell towards her making her jump and dance to avoid losing an eye and tearing an arm off her jacket in the process.

Forgetting its old-fashioned wooden solidity, she kicked the prostrate rack, hurting herself and probably scoring a massive bruise across her shin too.

Another string of curse words - just as well she had an "office" to herself and didn't have to contribute to anyone else's swear jar.

She picked her handbag out of the wreckage and left the cupboard, slamming the door behind her.

As she walked away, down the dim corridor, she heard something(s) crashing as it fell from the racks.

She paused for a moment, debating whether to go back and see what, then squared her shoulders, and kept walking, with no intention of returning.

No matter how curious she was about whether the door would actually open, or whether some brooding and unhappy presence had barricaded itself in.

Or her out.

Or whether she'd shot through the event horizon and out the other side into a universe very like the one she'd left only different in some way that wasn't readily apparent but would come to a horrifying conclusion over the next few weeks.

Honestly, the sooner she got back into less creative projects, the better. Something a little less creative and a little more stable and predictable.

Like construction.

But on her way off the lot, a sharp pain in her stomach reminded her she hadn't eaten in hours.

She stood still for a moment, one hand on her stomach trying to decide whether she could make it to the bus stop before passing out from hunger.

The lovely Art Deco café building on the main entrance to the back lot operated as an actual cafe, as well as a set, so she figured she might as well stop in on her way out and get herself one last discounted lunch.

To go.

But by the time she collected her chicken noodle soup and toasted ham and cheese sandwich, she knew she couldn't wait any longer, and found herself a sunbeam on the portico of a nearby building (currently dressed as a post office) to eat her sandwich.

She leaned back on a white painted pillar, stretched out her red denim jean clad legs, and tugged her white fitted button-down shirt down to a more comfortable fitting.

She couldn't remember which project was filming right now - something involving a pretty blonde boy and some kind of mixed martial arts fighting, currently rehearsing in and around a "bank" on the other side of the street.

Or maybe it was a shop.

They were still dressing the exterior, so it was hard to tell.

The men weren't fighting particularly fiercely, but the random sounds of grunting and limbs connecting was irritating and disturbing her attempt at calming herself sufficiently not to tear the head off the next person who spoke to her.

She pulled her phone and earbuds from their respective pockets in her handbag and plugged herself into something a little more calming and soothing.

Well, given it was a Stravinsky ballet, more like something loud and clashing, cleansing and cathartic.

It certainly added an unexpectedly dramatic dimension to the fight scene unfolding in front of her.

Though of course, it was carefully choreographed, which was why they were rehearsing.

And they were rehearsing for a movie, so what she was watching would come out something similar on the other side anyway.

But probably with a soundtrack leaning more towards the heavy metal end of the musical spectrum.

And when you thought about it, movies took a collection of singularly ordinary moments, shone a bit of gold light on them and undercut them with a bit of dramatic music and made them seem more exceptional than they really were.

Larger than life.

About six times larger on the smallest of theatre screens actually.

As many as thirty times on the larger.

Sandra closed her eyes, took a deep breath and held it for ten seconds before letting it out again.

She loosened the lid on her soup to let the steam out and give it some time to cool while she started eating her sandwich.

From her vantage point, Pretty Boy's fluid fighting style included the odd stylish gesture; he seemed sweet and wholesome, and she guessed he was playing the hero.

His dark-haired opponent's style was sparer and more calculated, suggesting a lethal efficiency, and she guessed he was the villain.

Despite herself, she was intrigued, and wondered why it was that she preferred the villain. Was it a kindred recognition of a different kind of precision to her own?

Or was it the sense that heroes live in a slightly parallel universe of sunshine and unceasing positivity, while villains see the universe for the miserable, dark place it is.

Was it possible the villain and hero were different sides of the same coin - light and dark, locked forever in mortal combat that neither of them would ever win?

The same guy spinning endlessly in battle with his own shadow.

Or more likely, it was time to give Stravinsky a break and listen to something more cheerful.

She shook her head to dispel her thoughts, and as she did, a drop of fat from her sandwich escaped the paper it was wrapped in and dripped onto her shirt.

She held her arms out to the side as she looked down on her chest.

Just bloody perfect.

Not only would everyone be staring at her breasts for the rest of the day, but she'd be tormented by the smell of toasted cheese.

And of course, she'd ruined her jacket so unless she went back to her office, tore the other arm off it, and wore it backwards, she was stuck like this.

And just when she thought her day couldn't get any worse, the fighting crossed the street, and Pretty Boy tripped over her outstretched legs and somehow kicked her soup all over her shirt too.

Unbelievable day.

"What the hell do you think you are doing?" he demanded. "Can't you see we're rehearsing here?"

After a moment of incredulity, Sandra struggled to her feet, flicking hot soup from her hands, before scraping it off her top, and accidentally on purpose flicking it in his direction.

"Actually," she said, crossing her arms over her nearly transparent shirt, "if you were rehearsing according to the approved protocols, you would have cleared the area, installed warning placards and the authorised safety barriers to prevent incidents like this.

"Clearly you're not rehearsing, you've just crossed the street to assault me."

Pretty Boy performed an unnecessarily flamboyant backflip back to his feet while Sandra took a step closer to the edge of the portico, to prevent him from stepping up to her level and towering over her.

He was tall enough as he was thank you very much.

She wondered if she remembered enough Taekwondo to get herself out of trouble, and as she thought about it, relaxed into position ready to strike.

As if in recognition, a hand fell on her shoulder at the same moment as a male voice from behind her said, "Oh my god, I'm so sorry about Jason, are you okay?"

She twisted out from under the hand and found herself face to chest with the villain, who was looking down into her face.

On the bright side, the cheese stain was indistinguishable from the soup stains, and he was looking at her face, not her chest.

She took a step back along the edge of the step, trying to maintain a safe distance from both of them, but the villain took a step closer to bridge the gap.

On the bright side, he was between her and Pretty Boy, or Jason, or whatever the hell his name was, and on the less bright side, he was still looking at her.

Sandra brought her feet together and stood as tall as she could without standing on her toes, "I'm fine, though it seems I am destined to be hungry today."

It seemed she might also be destined to never regain her composure.

"I don't know what you're apologising for Dan," Pretty Boy said, "placard schmacard, we have every right to be here."

Without breaking eye contact with her, Dan held up the palm of his hand back in Jason's direction.

"No, she's right. You could've been injured, and that could have delayed the shoot. Next time we'll do it properly."

She had the curious feeling Dan was trying to protect Pretty Boy from her.

While the thought she might capable of damaging him was amusing, it was just another reminder of how much working at Gorgon Studios sucked.

The only reason movie stars thought the world revolved around them was that for three months of filming it actually did.

They had to be kept happy so they didn't interrupt the schedule, that time and cost could be controlled, and hopefully, The Project brought in on time and on budget.

She sighed.

That was what she managed the schedules for after all.

That was why they all took care of the stars because with their faces plastered all over the screens, they were more or less irreplaceable for the duration whereas every other one of them was expendable.

She turned her back on Dan and picked up her bag and collected the remains of her lunch, "you take care of The Star, I'll get someone to clean up."

Back straight, head high, she walked away from the jerks.

Stopping to throw the remains of her lunch in a bin, and at the gatehouse to ask Sol to call for a cleaner, and then at the bus stop until a bus arrived.

Exit stage right.

«« • »»

Dan watched the girl go.

She was magnificent.

He'd been worried for a moment when Jason opened his stupid mouth, and he recognised her Taekwondo relax.

Though if he had to lay a bet on the outcome, her lightness and speed would've seen Jason rolling on the ground with a broken nose.

And the last thing they needed was a hero with a broken nose. Heroes were supposed to be pretty and virtuous, not scarred for life.

If they were being honest, Jason wasn't smart enough to play a villain, and he wasn't nice enough for anyone to take a chance on him - when he lost his looks, he'd lose his career as well.

Assuming the drugs didn't kill it first.

But that was Jason's problem, not his.

Though the idea of that girl, whoever she was, ending his career was delicious.

With a few weeks of filming left, there was enough time to come up with an idea of how he could make it happen.

He wouldn't be the only one happy to see Jason taken down a few pegs.

For the next few days, everywhere he went on the lot, he looked for her with no success.

He was reduced to asking questions, and after a while, he discovered Sandra Lockwood was one of the Studio schedulers.

And seemingly a very good one.

People who worked with her praised her efficiency and can-do attitude. People who didn't talked about how polite she was and how pleasant to be around.

So far as Dan could tell, the only person who had anything bad to say about her was Jason, which was as good a recommendation as any.

But apparently, she'd been ill, and no one had seen her for a while.

Once he knew who she was, it was easy to find her office. And once he'd seen her office, it was easy to see why she was ill.

Though Dan suspected there was more to it than just that.

What few knew, was that with 52% ownership, Dan was Gorgon Studios' senior partner.

He'd set up the studios with some help from his friends, primarily as a way to ensure he had work. And when he didn't, he at least had some money coming in.

They'd started out small, bought some derelict factories, hired some incredibly gifted people, and grown into a sought-after provider of backlot, sound stages, props and production services.

And given most people are nervous around bosses, especially more senior ones, Dan preferred to keep his ownership a secret because he got better results that way.

The question became, how did he get Sandra back to work where he could spend time with her without her knowing he was technically her boss.

And one of the stars of the movie, which might be even worse.

It seemed the best way was to check on her using the Jason incident as an excuse.

Which was how he came to be knocking on her apartment door with a bunch of flowers.

And when she opened the door, she really did look ill.

Pale face, limp hair, dark panda eyes.

Dan wasn't sure whether to hold his arms out to catch her or call an ambulance.

He held out the flowers instead.

She looked at them, she looked at him, and then shrugged and took them out of his hands and walked back inside.

But she didn't shut the door in his face, so he closed the door behind him.

The warm clove-scented room he followed her into was small, neat and clean. Plain white shelves disappeared into the white walls so that the few books and brightly coloured ornaments on display appeared to float in the air.

It was stark, but it was also strangely relaxing.

No extraneous clutter, nothing to suggest any other occupants.

Even the bright orange blanket she'd probably climbed out from underneath looked like art thrown back against the square deep blue couch it rested on.

Not to mention the low black lacquerware table.

Her dark, disorganised office must be a daily torture compared to this open and organised space.

"I heard you were ill," he said, "and I was worried Jason had hurt you."

He thought he heard her snort, but her head was in a cupboard so he couldn't say for sure.

She came out with a large vase and some scissors and started trimming the flowers to fit the vase.

"Not physically," she replied, "it was just one of those days."

"Why, what happened?"

She smiled slightly, "too stupid to go into."

Her eyes met his for a moment before bouncing away.

"Are you okay, you seem..." he waved his arms his vaguely, not wanting to say the words out loud.

She bent her face towards the flowers and sniffed them, the reds and yellows reflecting a healthy glow onto her face.

"I'm just tired."

"I called by your office, so I'm not surprised you're tired."

She frowned.

"Well, you live here, and the place you work couldn't be more different than this."

She looked around her as if she'd only just made the connection.

"I suppose that's true."

"When I get back to the lot, I'll tell them to clear the space up."

"Don't bother, I'm not planning to go back."

"You're not going to quit over Jason are you?"

"What? No, not him. He's just the last straw."

"Then what?"

"It's just time to move on."

"Surely there's more to it than that?"

"Yes. No. Oh, I don't know. The idea of returning just fills me with despair."

"Despair? That seems like a fairly strong reaction."

"You said you saw my office, right?"

He took a step towards her, "give me a chance to set this right."

"Give you a chance? I think you might be giving yourself a little too much credit, don't you?"

"I'm sorry, I feel like this is all my fault for letting Jason get out of control—"

She folded her arms across her chest, "I told you this isn't about Jason."

He risked another step forward, "then what?"

She looked at him for a long moment, and he thought she was going to throw him out with some choice words.

She sighed and sort of collapsed in on herself, "it just feels like this is one of those points where life could go either way. That the rest of my life depends on this decision."

Despite himself, he was intrigued. "this would be something related to your Taekwondo training?"

She laughed, "ah, you saw that did you?"

"I did. I would've put money on you to win - that's why I had to intervene."

"That's flattering, I guess.

"And yes, my mind is not at peace."

"Would you like to tell me about it? I can't promise wise counsel, but it might help you clarify your thoughts."

She did her Taekwondo relax for a moment as she stared at him for an eternity, before asking, "would you like some tea?"

Of course he nodded.

She didn't say anything as she boiled the kettle and prepared the tea things. She put them on a tray, and carried it over to the table, gesturing for him to sit as she knelt before the table and poured the tea.

She waited for him to take his first sip, and then she started talking.

He watched her face move as she spoke and admired the sparkle in her dark eyes.

A lock of her fringe fell forward and caught in her eyebrow, and he admired its tenacity.

He noticed her square, even teeth, and her thin pale lips.

And the less he listened to her words, and the more he admired her look, the more he understood that she was bored at work, and felt under-appreciated.

That she felt some guy had used their friendship, and ultimately her to achieve his own goals.

That she was better than this, and deserved more, but didn't quite know what she needed to do to get there.

Now and again, he poured her more tea and admired the economy of her movements as she drank it.

And couldn't help wondering how that would translate to her bedroom before forcing himself back to the matter at hand.

Eventually, she ran out of words.

He said nothing.

She reached into the sleeve of her shirt, pulled out a scrunched-up tissue and blew her nose.

"How do you feel?" he asked.

She smiled, "better."

"Want some advice?"

"No. But I'll give you a second chance."

"Me?"

"I know who you are Daniel Carruthers, movie star and Gorgon Studios CEO."

"Ah," he laughed a little nervously.

"I'll be back at work next week. Show me what you've got."

«« • »»

Sandra stood across the road, looking at the studio's main entrance.

There was nothing obviously different, but there was some kind of subtle change in the air.

A kind of lightness.

Not cheerfulness exactly, but a kind of airiness.

Like after a thunderstorm when the first few sunbeams shine through the departing clouds.

Clean and bright.

Or maybe it was just her.

The café seemed livelier, and her takeout latte was delivered in her reusable cup with a smiley face drawn on the lid.

As she made her way across the lot, she was surprised and touched by the number of people who stopped to greet her, to tell her they'd missed seeing her about the place and were glad she was back.

She'd never felt like a part of the place before.

No sign of Dan though.

Not sure whether she was glad about that or not.

Not that she was looking, she told herself.

Her corridor looked the same, her office door looked the same.

Maybe a little cleaner.

She put her hand on the knob and paused before turning it, but had no sense of an unhappy brooding presence.

She flung the door open and was confronted by clean white walls.

The window had been replaced, and the new one was not only clean but open a crack to let fresh air in and the hint of paint out.

Under the window, an orange couch snuggled with a blue rug under a silver-coloured lamp stand topped with a white shade.

And behind the couch, a large, framed, orange-tinted movie poster for *The Day the Schedule Broke*, starring Sandra Lockwood and Dan Carruthers. It showed Dan crouching before a taller, somewhat menacing version of her, arms spread wide in defence of a cowering Jason.

It reminded her a little of the original *Attack of the 50 ft Woman* poster.

To her left, the racking remained, though painted white, and aside from some files and empty space, it contained several bright green plants in white pots.

On her right, diagonally opposite the door, a long, pale wood table took up almost the entire wall. One end was topped with neat stacks of colour coded, sticky noted, highlighted and marked-up schedule pages, the other held a new black computer and printer.

And in the middle, a wide-open space for laying out the plans. Under the desk, under the stacks of paper, was a low lateral filing cabinet.

A wheeled office chair, matching the orange couch sat between the table and the wall, giving her easy access to the long whiteboard hung on the wall, currently showing a Gantt chart of the main studio schedule.

She took a step into the room and shut the door.

Behind the door, a coat rack was screwed to the wall. And on the rack, in a plastic dry-cleaning shroud, hung a jacket. It looked a lot like her old jacket, with the sleeve sewn back on.

She smiled.

The room was perfect.

And she wondered if all that space had been there all along, or if Dan'd moved the walls.

She hung her bag and the jacket she was wearing on the rack, turned her computer on, and sat swinging from side to side on the new chair, sipping her coffee, while she waited for a gazillion new emails to download.

But she found herself distracted by the movie poster, and took her coffee to stand in front of it, examining it closely.

Jason's screwed up terrified face, Dan's dropped jaw and wide, staring eyes, her own scowling face as she waved a sandwich menacingly at the puny creatures cowering before her. A tiny overturned bowl of soup on the steps.

It was ingenious, and to be honest, a bit flattering too.

"So how did I do?" he asked from behind her.

"I love it," she said, turning around, arm brushing across his chest as she found him closer than expected.

And dressed better, in a dark suit, shirt and tie.

"Wrapping up filming?"

"Nah, board meeting."

She snorted, "you look nice."

"Nice enough to take you out for a drink?"

"I just got here! And it's not even lunchtime yet."

"You're late. And it's nearly lunchtime. Though I should get back to the meeting."

He held a hand out to her, "meet later?"

Surprising herself as well as him, she took his hand, "okay."

He held her gaze for a moment before kissing the back of her hand, "I'll look forward to it."

She blushed like a schoolgirl as she watched him leave, his aftershave lingering behind him.

Didn't seem like she'd broken his schedule, though hers might never recover.

She bounced on the balls of her feet a few times, before jumping and spinning, and lashing out into the empty space with a head-height kick.

It seemed things were taking a turn for the better.

She couldn't wait to see him again.

THE END

ALEXANDRIA
BLAELOCK
AUTHOR OF FATE IN YOUR HANDS
MORNING STAR
EVENING STAR
SUPERSTAR
A SHORT STORY

MORNING STAR, EVENING STAR, SUPERSTAR

Hunter Preston strode, buck naked, through the wide-open glass back doors of his house, stretched and roared in the Summer sunshine.

Then ran the last few steps across the stoned patio toward his sparkling clean swimming pool, jumped, and pulling his knees towards his chest, did a massive bombie into the pool.

Christy did a double-take and nearly fell out of her tree.

She scrabbled at the jacaranda's dry, scratchy bark, trying to keep her place. Grateful for the slight protection her threadbare jeans and long-sleeved t-shirt offered.

She looked through the view-finder again. Barracuda of the Business World indeed!

Quite a contrast from the urbane and sophisticated gentleman in perfectly fitted tux she'd photographed at last week's launch banquet.

Or the dark and dangerous man straddling his Ducati in tight blue jeans and a black leather jacket mid-week.

But not so different from yesterday's lithe and sporty footballer playing in the charity match.

She liked what she'd seen of him, not just physically, but the courteous way he interacted with people around him too.

As if he didn't think he was someone special.

And in the league of super-rich arseholes, that did make him someone special.

She sighed and leaned her forehead against the tree trunk.

She'd make more money selling these pictures to a nudie magazine, but even though she'd stooped as low as taking paparazzo style photos, she'd signed an exclusive contract and wasn't going to break it.

Though it wouldn't do his reputation any harm, and she could do with the extra money.

Freelancing was hard enough, what with photos of pretty much anything you like freely available on the Internet.

It was a sad indictment of the state of the world that the most reliable and well-paid work was private investigation.

And that's a dirty business at the best of times, so she wasn't going to make it any dirtier.

Not that she knew what was going to happen to her photos, but she trusted Mack not to get her into any sticky situations.

Hopefully, whoever was buying was going to respect Hunter's privacy and not on-sell them either.

But right now, she hoped he'd quickly retire to his million-dollar heritage-listed mansion so she could leave without detection.

Slight though she was, her precarious perch was uncomfortable, and the sight of his luscious body was making her light-headed.

Or maybe that was not having eaten breakfast.

Not to mention the thought of his lean, hard body against hers was making her heart race so fast she thought she might have a heart attack.

Though there wasn't much chance of him seeing her, let alone touching her.

She snapped off another couple of pictures, tempted to keep one or two for herself.

There's no harm in dreaming about what you can't have. And he'd be a great addition to her vision board.

But even if she could have him, there's no way he'd slot neatly into her life.

Even if he wanted to.

She heard a slight noise and looked down. It was a big fluffy golden retriever snuffling around the base of the tree. It looked up at her and whined softly.

More likely he'd dominate her life, and she'd find herself slotting into his.

Like this cutie.

"Nice doggy, go away."

It wagged its tail.

"Go away," she hissed, making shooing motions, "I don't want Him over here, checking what you're doing."

It jumped on its hind legs bracing its body against the tree and woofed up at her.

A quick glance assured her that Hunter, sporting in the pool, hadn't yet noticed his dog's preoccupation, so she risked leaning over to scratch its head.

Too late she realised she was slipping and grappled frantically with thin air to save herself.

She crashed to the ground, fortunately, cushioned by a lush manicured lawn, the breath leaving her lungs in a whoosh.

There was no time to recover, for the dog was on her, trying to crawl through her arms to lick her face.

She rolled over to escape it and heard the sickening crunch as she crushed her camera before she felt the stab of pain.

She gave in and let the dog lick her.

Now she had no camera, and the fate of the SD card was doubtful. Would there be any salvageable images?

This was what happened when you got greedy.

It wasn't very professional to break your equipment while being tickled to death by a dog.

Squeezing her eyes shut to hold back the tears she thought of all the bills waiting to be paid.

She was so tired of struggling.

"Biscuit, what do you think you are doing?"

The dog backed up and sat down, leaving her a clear view of Hunter's strong, square face.

His crystal blue eyes seemed to bore right through her and out the other side.

Not the most comfortable thought.

"Ah, another tourist who got lost."

He leaned down and grabbed her hand, pulling her to her feet, less roughly than she'd expected.

He held her hand for a fraction of a second too long as he continued his intense searching look.

Did she have something on her face?

She dragged her forearm across her face just in case.

He grinned down at her, revealing even white teeth, then nonchalantly brushed a few flecks of grass off her shoulders.

The small towel draped demurely around his waist, emphasised his slim hips and highlighted rows of muscles on muscles on muscles.

Not really a barracuda.

More like a puma, trussed up for its visit with the zoo vet.

He flicked his damp hair off his face with a toss of his head.

"I can see you're a photographer, but who are you, and why are you here?"

She squared her shoulders and stood as tall as she could to minimise their height difference.

Under other circumstances, she'd fit snugly under his arm, but she tried to banish the thought and concentrate on the conversation.

"My name is Christy Zachary, and I'm with Underground Investigations."

"Christy Zachary, hmmmmmm..."

"Didn't you do a spread about street kids a few years ago?"

"Um, well, yes."

She was surprised he remembered it. It'd been a big thing, quickly dropped in favour of more pleasant topics.

"Times are obviously hard if you're in investigations."

"Well..."

"Okay, who sent you?"

"I don't know, I just take the pictures."

"Probably just my ex-wife then," he gave her a crocodile smile.

"Do you have enough pictures, or would you like me to pose for some more?"

His hands slipped down towards the towel.

She blushed and backed away, waving her hands as a barrier in front of her, "no no no, thanks, I'm fine."

"Oh look, you broke your camera. Maybe we should schedule for a more suitable time, when you have your spare."

"No, really, it'll be fine."

"Well, come along then, and I'll show you out. Unless you'd care to climb the fence again?"

She crouched to pick up the pieces of her camera, hoping she could salvage some of it and tried not to catch his smiling eyes as he looked over his shoulder to make sure she was following.

What exactly did he find amusing about this situation?

There was clearly a lot more to him than the domineering businessman portrayed by the press.

Soon enough she was on the other side of the fence, slightly consoled by Biscuit's lingering kiss.

She ignored the security guard and leant on the wall trying to catch her breath.

Well, trying not to cry actually.

The pieces in her arms were her spare camera, and she couldn't afford to buy another.

And you can't be a photographer if you don't have the tools of the trade.

«« • »»

Somehow Hunter managed to get back inside the house before he started laughing.

Christy Zachary, currently from Underground Investigations, was like an adorably angry kitten. Green eyes wide, arched back, black hair on end, hissing.

He wanted to play that kitten game where you try to tickle her belly without getting scratched, but he had the feeling he'd have to be pretty fast.

Grabbing a beer from the fridge on the way, he stripped off his towel and went back outside to sunbake on it.

Biscuit climbed up on the lounger, and after turning in a circle, lay down at his feet with her chin on his ankle.

Christy Zachary couldn't be that bad if his cranky old dog liked her.

And now that he thought about it, what was that stupid magazine that wanted to run a story on him? Man something?

He'd insist they use her.

He eased himself out from under Biscuit and went to make a few calls.

«« • »»

Back in her empty apartment, Christy discovered neither the lense nor the camera could be saved.

Though she managed to pull a few pics from the card and get them off to Mack with some of the previous.

That at least would bring a few hundred in.

Which would help, because she'd already sold everything of value, including her best cameras.

She still had her phone, of course, and those pictures would be fine for some kinds of jobs.

But the fancy camera was not just a tool of trade, it was a credential too.

In the meantime, she checked to find no new orders and no suitable new jobs. She crossed her fingers and sent off a few overdue account emails because that was at least doing something.

If her life continued along this vein, it wouldn't be long before she'd have to start redefining her hard nos.

Or reconsider life as a supermarket checkout chick.

She flopped on the couch, pulled her pink plaid blanket up to her chin and spent the next few days sleeping to escape from her problems.

She knew she had to do something, but she couldn't bear to think about it.

Something would happen to save her; she just didn't know what yet.

«« • »»

Hunter knocked again on the weathered apartment door. So hard he thought it might come off its hinges. If she didn't answer soon, he wasn't sure what he was going to do.

He was just about to knock again when it opened a crack to reveal Christy's squinting eye half covered by a tousled lock of black hair in some kind of anime cuteness.

After a moment, when she didn't say anything, he pushed the door open to reveal a small dishevelled woman in a stained oversize t-shirt. One who'd clearly just got off the shabby little couch.

Which was a little funny given how much time he'd spent changing his clothes in the hopes of impressing her.

Google had been surprisingly unhelpful on the topic of what to wear to commission an artist.

And now that he was here, the charcoal suit matched with a white and blue striped shirt, socks and tie, plus gleaming white gold accessories seemed a bit overdone.

Especially given that the couch was one of two pieces of furniture in the tiny but neat studio apartment, the other being a low table.

Dammit, why did she make him feel a teenager who was trying too hard?

"Nice place you have here."

Christy snorted and rubbed the sleep from her eyes.

He held out a gift-wrapped box, "I bought you a new camera."

She didn't look at the box, just screwed her eyes up to look at him, perhaps seeking a different f/stop.

"I don't know what to say."

He grinned, "thank you would be a good start."

"Oh, sorry," she blushed and looked away, "thank you very much."

"That's better. Now you ask me if I'd like some coffee."

She filled an old kettle with water and turned it on before rinsing some chipped cups from the drainer and spooning instant coffee into the cups.

She didn't look like much of a morning person, and he wondered whether he might have been better off bringing her coffee than a camera.

"You don't believe much in worldly goods, do you?"

"I'm not here much, not that it's any of your business."

"But it is, I'm a prospective employer."

She made a face after sniffing the milk and put it back in the tiny fridge on the bench.

"I was quite impressed by your street life spread, and some of your other work. You've a knack for bringing out the best in your subjects.

"And when *Metropolitan Man* magazine approached me for an interview, I said I wouldn't do it unless you took the pictures."

The kettle clicked off, so she poured the water into the cups, offering him black with no sugar before taking a sip of her own.

"You're insane, they'll never agree."

"They already did. They'll be in touch shortly."

Somewhere her phone rang with a cartoon theme tune he vaguely recognised before cutting out.

"Seeing as you don't currently have a camera, it seemed a good idea to get you one."

"What? How did you know that?"

"Well, in my position a few discreet enquiries are in order."

"But why me?"

He put the cup on the table without taking a sip.

"Leaving aside your undeniable talent, you won't be obtrusive, and if anyone notices you, you'll look good following me around.

"But—"

"Look, all you have to do is follow me around taking photos, it's what you've been doing for the last few weeks after all."

"Yes, but-"

He looked at his watch, "I've got to get to the office now, but one of my assistants will be here shortly to give you a hand with your wardrobe selection."

"But—"

"Good, I'm glad that's settled." He shook her limp hand, "I'll see you later this afternoon."

And then he left, trying to smother his self-satisfied smile.

That went better than expected.

He couldn't wait to see if she arrived.

《《 • 》》

Oh.

My.

God.

As if the lingering scent of Hunter's woody cologne wasn't enough, now she was trying to wrangle Justin, the immaculately turned out Queer Eye.

Who'd gone all bug-eye.

His horror at the state of her wardrobe, more empty capsule than wardrobe, must surely be audible six blocks away.

Any minute now her downstairs neighbours would be banging on their roof with a broomstick to tell her to quieten down.

Not that he was squawking for nothing.

It was some time since she'd had the kind of well-paid open and above-board gigs that required decent clothes rather than undercover work up trees and behind parked cars.

And damn him, Justin was right, she was on a downward spiral.

And something needed to be done.

And yes, new clothes were an investment in her future.

She allowed herself to be dragged to the waiting limousine with the minimum of protest, mainly because she was trying to calculate the maximum she could afford to spend.

Their first stop was a shoe store where he chose some ridiculously expensive black ballet flats for her to try on.

"They're beautiful," she breathed, "but way too expensive."

"Try walking around. Are they comfortable? "Do they rub?"

She walked a few paces then crouched, and stretched, and climbed on the chairs.

"They're fine. Perhaps perfect."

"So, after an eight-hour day of following and photographing Mr Preston, you'll still be standing?"

Christy bounced a couple of times to try them out, "yes, I think so. But I can't afford them."

"Goodness, were you not listening when I talked about investing in yourself?"

"Yes, but—"

Justin pulled a plain black credit card from his back pocket and waggled it in her face. "Mr Preston has authorised me to cover your reasonable expenses for your assignment."

"These shoes, delightful as they are, are not reasonable expenses."

"Christy, Christy, Christy," he said, shaking his head. "In this instance, I am the sole arbiter of what are reasonable expenses, and I will brook no argument from you."

She made another feeble attempt at protest, and he dragged her to a nearby full-length mirror.

And pointed at the woman who looked as though she'd just crawled out from underneath a newspaper blanket behind a commercial rubbish skip.

"Take a long hard look at yourself woman."

He took his phone from his jacket pocket and opened a calendar app. "This week alone, Mr Preston has three board meetings, a government consultative committee, a TV interview, and a charity dinner at a high-end hotel.

"Are you telling me this vagrant," he gestured at the mirror, "will be permitted to enter any of these places?"

She made a doubtful face.

"Do you have any concept of the harm you could do to his reputation dressing like a tramp and trailing around after him trying to take his picture?"

She winced as his barbs drove home and shook her head.

"And what about your reputation?"

She shrunk a little smaller.

"Will you accept my judgement in this matter?"

She nodded.

Justin, fully vindicated, smiled beatifically, and pulled out another couple of pairs of shoes for her to try.

Over the next few hours, she followed him from store to store, tried on all the clothes and lingerie he offered and accepted his verdict without comment.

The black card got such a workout she wondered how it wasn't smoking.

She didn't complain when he took her to an up-market Japanese restaurant for lunch.

Or when he left her at a Beauty Salon for a massage and makeover. Or when he told her what to put on when she was done.

And when she couldn't find the clothes she'd arrived in, she decided not to ask.

«« • »»

At first, Hunter didn't notice the woman taking photographs.

She discreetly drifted around the floor, pointing her camera down corridors, at windows and him.

He only noticed her because he was on the phone, staring through his glass office wall, and she happened to be the only thing moving at the time.

It took him a moment to recognise the elegant woman in skinny black jeans, a lightly fitted black silk shirt, flat black shoes, and a long silver chain.

As she turned her head, he saw her hair was caught up in a loose bun held together by chopsticks, and he wanted to pull them out and thread his fingers through it as he kissed her.

So intensely, she'd forget everything else.

She wasn't an angry kitten anymore; she'd become something infinitely more beautiful and much more dangerous; a black panther.

Even worse, a panther he'd invited to stalk and capture him.

The call ended, but he kept the phone at his ear, an excuse to watch her slowly raise her camera to her face and press the shutter release in his direction.

God help him.

Would the pictures show how incredibly attractive he found her?

He licked his lips.

Would there be a difference now they both knew who the buyer was?

«« • »»

She felt weirdly sexy in her black photographer's outfit. Or maybe sexy wasn't the right word, maybe it was confident.

Capable.

In control

Bold.

She locked eyes with Hunter as she raised the camera towards him.

The world shrunk to his tiny image reflected in the window.

He licked his lips and turned to face her.

She heard something break inside her.

Was it her self-control?

She took a few shots.

Maybe she wasn't in control, maybe she was just shameless.

She lowered the camera and took a step towards his office.

He put the phone down and rose from his chair.

Still meeting her eyes.

Maybe being dominated by him wouldn't be so bad if that was what it took to feel like a sexy grown-the-hell-up woman.

She took another step, and he walked around his desk.

How long before he left her a puddle of mush as he walked away looking for someone more exciting than her?

Did it matter?

At least he wouldn't take all her cash with him when he left.

She'd be left with money in the bank, clothes in her closet, and a corridor of doors opening in his wake.

Another step brought her to his office door.

He sat on the edge of his desk, waiting to see what she'd do next.

What the hell, she'd think of reasons why not later.

She stepped into the room, shutting the door behind her and leaning on it.

He pointed a remote to trigger the privacy frosting, then walked over to kiss her.

Thoroughly.

Deeply.

As if she was the only woman on the planet.

«« • »»

The kiss was better than he'd imagined.

And Christy didn't scratch him.

Her soft, warm body seemed to melt into his, and her hair, when he set it free was smooth and silky as it slid through his fingers. He was drowning in her light floral fragrance.

How could one woman have snared him so completely with so little effort?

He broke off the kiss, but she stood on tiptoe to capture him again.

This was no good, he had to tell her the truth before it got out of hand. He gently pushed her away.

"There's almost nothing I'd rather do than be kissed senseless by you, but I have a confession to make."

She looked up at him from dazed eyes.

He groaned and forced himself to guide her across to the conversational side of his office where he sat her on a couch and poured her a glass of water.

She took a couple of sips and seemed better able to string together coherent thoughts, which was more than he could say for himself.

He turned his back on her, and paced the length of his office, trying to work out how to tell her.

An action that seemed to annoy her as she snapped, "All right, out with it."

And given he'd been a hair's breadth from losing control and devouring her on the couch she sat on, it seemed a reasonable response.

"Argh." he started.

"I knew who you were all along, and I was the one who hired you to take the pictures of me."

She looked at him, took a sip of water, and put the glass down on the coffee table.

He didn't know if she was thinking, or trying to say something, or just wondering if he was some kind of stalker psycho.

"I just wanted to meet you, and it seemed like there was no other way."

He felt like he was losing his edge, so he flopped on the couch beside her and took her hand.

"Why aren't you saying anything?"

"Well, it's not like you've given me much of an opportunity yet."

"What are you thinking?"

She scratched her head, "I'm just wondering when, and how, and why me."

"Okay, well, um, you're an amazing artist, and I love your work, and I wanted to meet you, and when I found out you weren't taking commissions or doing events, I did some research and found out that hiring the investigator was about the only way I could hire you, and maybe meet you, and I thought I'd just book in and see what happened and maybe—"

He forced his mouth to close before he could look like even more of an idiot than he already did.

And when he dared to meet her eyes, they were dancing, she snorted, "Barracuda of the Business World indeed."

He smiled a little, and when he realised he still had her hand, a little more.

"Are you seriously telling me you've gone as giddy as a school girl because you're meeting me?"

He giggled.

Oh my god he giggled!

What the hell was wrong with him?

She laughed.

And laughed and laughed.

And when it seemed like she couldn't laugh any more, took a deep breath and gasped, "I'm sorry," before laughing some more.

Fanning her red face with her spare hand.

And when she could breathe again, she grabbed his face and kissed him.

"Let's get out of here," she said.

«« • »»

Christy lay on a lounger, reading the *Metropolitan Man* article, Biscuit by her side.

With a whoop, Hunter bolted from the house and landed with an enormous splash in the pool.

She lowered the magazine to watch him swim back towards her and crawl up the stairs to shake the water off on her.

Biscuit growled half-heartedly and retreated back into the house.

She smiled up at him, wondering which of them had been more nervous about meeting the big celebrity other.

He eased into the vacant space beside her and dropped a kiss on her lips.

Not that it mattered anymore, they'd met, and all that remained was the rest of their lives.

THE END

ALEXANDRIA
BLAELOCK
AUTHOR OF FATE IN YOUR HANDS
SHINING STAR
A SHORT STORY

SHINING STAR

"And this is Jason Winter who'll be playing the male lead General Chang."

I'll be honest.

I hadn't been paying attention.

I'm the author of best-selling novel *Bayside Bloodshed*, and it's being made into a movie.

Yay me!

We authors can be a bit precious about our books, so we aren't usually invited to any cast or crew meetings.

I should have been more grateful and involved, but the Director had said something about a local archaeological dig, and it set my train of thought heading to a different station.

Could I send my hero General Chang to the pyramids?

I was staring out the window at a morning sky so blue and sunny I could almost smell the gum trees and nibbling at some kind of sweet pastry as I tried to work through how I'd get him there.

And what he might do when he got there.

I was slightly annoyed when my train got derailed.

Schooling my face into a polite smile, I turned to greet the star and gasped as I looked up at the General himself.

I mean really, Jason was exactly what I'd imagined as I wrote Chang.

Dark eyes with ridiculously long lashes, dark hair, clean-shaven, lovely long pointy sideburns.

Tight t-shirt revealing just enough lean muscle in all the right places.

What was worse, he smiled Chang's sardonic smile, seeming to understand my shock and surprise.

As if it happened *all* the time.

My stomach lurched, and for an instant, I thought I might throw up on him.

He held out his hand to shake.

I transferred the pastry to my left hand, wiped my sticky right one down the leg of my jeans and offered it to him.

His hand was warm and soft as it enfolded mine. He smelled of sandalwood soap.

Just like Chang.

Did he do it deliberately?

"Ms Mason," he said in a rich baritone, bowing his head a little, "pleased to meet you.

"I haven't read your book, but I've heard it's good. I'm looking forward to bringing Chang to life".

I swallowed.

So far as I could tell, he was doing an excellent job so far, but he was making me very uncomfortable.

And he didn't seem in any hurry to let my hand go.

Which was fantastic!

But I was starting to hyperventilate and didn't think passing out at his feet would be a good look.

I had to get away.

At last my Celebrity Author Persona clicked into place, "I'm sure you'll do well Mr Winter, I look forward to seeing your interpretation."

I tried to pull my hand back, but he held it firmly, pinning me in place with his gaze.

Like an ugly moth mounted on a dusty museum board in an antique cupboard.

He was going to make one hell of a General Chang.

Fortunately, the Director forced him to let me go by introducing me to the female lead - the Poor Girl didn't stand a chance against Chang.

I said something suitably encouraging (at least I hope so).

I'm often at functions making inane small talk with readers, but not usually with my back to a long streak of gorgeousness.

Thankfully it was soon time to leave the actors to their first rehearsal, and the Director handed me over to the Producer to introduce me to the crew.

I couldn't help myself but look back as I walked through the door, and Chang, I mean Winter, was smiling slightly as he watched me leave.

I tripped over my feet as I exited stage left.

So.

Not.

Cool.

The Producer, it turned out, had read the book. In fact, he loved it so much he was probably the reason it was now going into production.

I left my foolish starstruck writer in the corridor, firmly buttoned Celebrity Author Persona up to my chin, and set myself to charming the pants off him and the crew.

I signed copies of the book and told them a little about how the idea came to me, and the story grew.

We walked around the half-constructed sound stage, and they explained how the sets and rigs would be put together.

It was fun, and really much more interesting than I expected.

I asked lots of questions because you never know when some of this stuff might come in handy for a story.

And I had heaps of fun trying out some of the rigging.

I got the impression that a lot of people are more interested in the actors than the behind the scenes stuff, but when you think about it, you can't get much more behind the scenes than the writing.

These were more my people than the actors.

Several dirty but happy hours passed before I got the sense that it was time to leave, I wanted to play a bit longer, but it's always better to go out on a high.

The Producer escorted me to the main entrance and called for a car to take me back to my hotel.

I meant it sincerely when I thanked him for an exciting day and assured him I was fine to wait on my own.

I sprawled comfortably in a seat outside the empty reception room, legs outstretched, hands folded across my stomach, head leaning back.

My face was towards the sun, and I closed my eyes and took a deep breath of river scented air.

There was a lot to think about, and I wanted to re-board the Chang goes to Egypt train of thought before it left for good.

Not to mention enjoy some fresh air, and quiet time alone to recover from the day's event.

It's not a coincidence that writers are introverts.

But, no such luck.

The car that pulled up next to me was driven by none other than Jason Winter.

Who crawled out of the tiny red vintage E-type Jaguar convertible.

The same car I gave Chang.

"I'm heading in your direction, can I give you a lift?"

I really didn't want any more to do with Chang just then.

Five minutes on top of the months I'd spent in the visceral act of creating him was already too much for one lifetime.

I know that sounds contradictory given I was already thinking about his next adventure.

But in my defence, that was more along the lines of sending him out for groceries than sitting in a tiny space that was already too small to contain his essence, let alone me as well.

Might as well sit next to a time bomb waiting for it to go off.

"No thanks, a car's been ordered for me."

He leaned back against the front wing, crossing his legs and hooking his thumbs in his pockets.

"Well, actually, it hasn't. I overheard the order and cancelled it."

How rude!

"You'll be waiting a while if you don't come with me."

He drew on the ground with his toe and looked at me from lowered eyes in a head turned slightly away from me.

Classic Princess move.

It seemed I had no choice but to get into his absurdly tiny car.

Could I keep it professional?

He'd already seen me in my usual shambolically absent-minded writer guise.

Worth a try.

I reengaged the Celebrity Author Persona as I stood to walk to the car.

He bolted upright and turned to open the door for me.

Even worse, he offered his hand to hold as I collapsed into the car.

"So, how was your tour Ms Mason?" he asked as we drove off, roof folded back, down the highway into the sunset.

My long dark hair streamed behind me, and my writer's soul rebelled at the cliché.

Not to mention trying to ignore the heat radiating from his body.

The way he tossed his head to flick the hair out of his eyes.

And how he leaned a little towards me when he glanced at me as he asked the question.

"Oh, I enjoyed it immensely."

I groaned inwardly. Did I really say that?

What the hell (aside from Chang) was wrong with me?

Was it time to get real and drop the Celebrity Author Persona?

"Look, I'm sorry I sound like an idiot Mr Winter. I just can't see you through Chang."

He opened his mouth and took a breath to speak, but nothing came out.

He glanced at me, frowned a little and tried again.

Still nothing

"Do you know, I really don't know what to say to that."

"I guess there isn't anything you can say. It's like I've got you mixed up with your twin. You'll probably always be Chang to me."

Oops.

He smiled Chang's mocking smile again, "Well, perhaps you could start by calling me Jason."

Distracted by the sunlight glancing off the fine hairs on his forearms, I said "and you can call me Amy."

Oh my god, I'd told him my real name, not my pen name.

I mean really, what was wrong with me?

"Amy." The sound poured from his lips like a lovely drink of peaty Laphroaig whisky, and I felt a spark of excitement leap deep inside me.

Not Chang, I reminded myself, but I'm not sure either of us had a chance against the charismatic character I'd created.

I'd never expected to actually meet the man who lived inside my head.

"Yes Jason?"

"I think I'm going to have to buy your book."

"Are you sure it won't taint your performance?" Curious writer engaged for the moment.

"Maybe it will give me added depth."

"Well, I suppose at least you'll have a better idea of what he's thinking."

I let the Celebrity Author Persona take the lead again.

My poor writer's brain was miles away, already imagining what it would be like to stand on the red carpet with him at the film's premiere.

Wearing high heels with something long and shiny, feeling his arm tighten around my waist as he told reporters how much he loved my work.

In his deep sexy voice.

In between adoring gazes.

"Sorry, what was that?" I'd lost track of the actual conversation again.

I had to get rid of him before I started muttering the imaginary one.

"I said we're here."

"Oh, thanks! Look, if you want to read the book, I've a copy in my room you can have."

Oh well done Amy, now you'll never get rid of him.

"That's okay, the studio gave me one, I just didn't bother reading it."

Ouch!

I climbed out of the car, "Ah, Okay. Well, thanks for the ride Jason. Perhaps we'll meet again once day."

And I fled, like a coward, before I could let any-thing else slip.

Or him say anything for that matter.

Safely inside my overly luxurious production funded hotel suite, I poured myself a whisky (so I could drink the sound of his voice) and fired up my laptop.

Who exactly was this Jason Winter?

Well, it seemed he was famous.

Not that I should have been surprised about that.

He'd made a few critically acclaimed and highly popular action films, been nominated for a couple of awards and won one.

Was regularly seen about town with any number of pretty starlets.

(Why are they called starlets anyway, is it because despite appearances they're still babies?)

He was a couple of years younger than me, and grew up on a dairy farm in a country town.

He'd modelled a bit for pocket money at Agricul-tural College, and been "discovered" shooting a com-mercial for jeans.

He liked to go back to the farm periodically to "get back to his roots." He occasionally sang with his younger brother's band (who I had actually heard of and was a bit of a fangirl).

His favourite colour was blue, he had a cat, and he loved jam doughnuts.

Fascinating how much you can find out about someone on the net.

Whether any of it's true or not is another matter. After all, I'd been so disturbed about some of the things said about me that I'd given up googling myself and shut down all my Celebrity Author social media accounts.

I was tempted to check myself out for comparison, but a writer who wants to stay more or less sane never reads her reviews.

Instead, I poured myself another whisky and took it to the balcony door.

The city lights below me were bright enough to dim the stars above, and neon reflections flashed across the ceiling in a bright rainbow of colour.

I opened the door and walked out.

Setting my drink on the wrought iron table, I sat on one companion chair propping my feet on the other and listened to the sound of the night.

Seagulls squawking, people talking, car horns tooting on the street, fun and laughter in the hotel bar below.

My stomach grumbled. The complementary fruit basket wasn't what I was hungry for, so I grabbed my handbag and headed out.

We'd passed a noodle shop on the way back, and I had a sudden urge for spicy noodle soup.

But who should I meet as the elevator doors opened, but Jason Winter with a bag of something that smelled delicious.

"Amy! We meet again!"

I clutched my bag to my chest for protection, "Hello Jason, I was just on my way out."

"It's been a long day, and I thought you might be hungry."

"That's so sweet, but I'm off to see some local friends before I fly home tomorrow."

I'm a writer, I can lie with the best of them.

"Oh. Well, I wanted to apologise. I thought you might be offended when I dismissed your book offer."

"Well, um, thank you. That's very kind.

He jiggled the food bag, "Are you sure you have to go out?"

Time stood still for a moment as I stood drowning in his eyes.

Why not indulge the fantasy? It's not like I would ever see him (or Chang) again.

If I needed an excuse, I'd call it in-depth research.

Goodbye caution, have a good time with the wind.

"Okay, sure. It was more of an "if you're not busy" thing anyway."

I led him back down the corridor, acutely aware that he was following only a step or two behind, and trying not to sway my hips too provocatively.

I'm not sure I was successful.

Letting him in was a mistake.

As large as the suite was, he seemed to take up entirely too much of it, sucking all the oxygen out of it.

Even though I'd accidentally left the balcony door open.

Even though it was a bigger space than the car I'd recently escaped from.

The air was thick with seething untold stories and his sandalwood scent inescapable.

How could it be more intense now than when I first met him, what eight, ten hours ago?

I could hear ghostly echoes of him calling out my name in the throes of passion.

Hey wait a minute.

Who was calling my name?

Was it Jason, or was it Chang?

Did it matter?

Trying to pretend everything was fine, and that I wasn't living multiple lives simultaneously, I static-shocked us both as I brushed past him on my way back to the mini-bar.

And kicked my shoes off, hoping the smell of my feet wasn't stronger than his soap.

He said, "I didn't know what you'd like so I got noodle soup - plain or spicy, and all the sides. I hope that's ok."

Had I slipped into a parallel universe?

"I was just thinking about spicy noodle soup. Would you like to share?"

"Yes please, that one's my favourite."

He took a seat, started pulling food out of the bag and arranging it on the table.

I crouched inelegantly to pull a bottle of Sauvignon Blanc from the fridge (phew, feet fine) and brought it to the table with a couple of chilled glasses and a corkscrew.

He took the lids off the food containers, while I poured the wine.

After a short interlude of reason trying to reassert itself, I ignored it and sat in the chair next to him.

All the better to eat soup with.

I had this one night to live the life of one of my characters.

Tomorrow I'd be back at home, in my daggy track pants, accompanied only by my farty geriatric dog and overly vivid imagination.

This trip would fade to a dream, and I'd probably never see Jason Winter again, well not unless I watched the film.

And while I had a creative veto, I'm not sure I could sit through the result anyway.

Your critical voice can be a real killer.

He tapped a pack of chopsticks on the table to break it open, then handed it to me.

I watched him open his, his movements graceful and economical.

I wondered if he'd taken martial arts or dance classes as a child. Or was it just the result of chasing cows in the clean country air.

Right up until my fifth book sales went nuts, I'd been a City girl, so I had no idea.

I cut myself off as I started to imagine a romantic life on a farm with him.

That was a step too far.

I must have made some kind of vocalisation (not uncommon for a woman who lives alone, let alone one who writes) and he raised one eyebrow at me.

"Sorry, occupational hazard. When you're a writer, you're never really in touch with reality.

"And you're almost always talking to imaginary friends."

Wow, I'd really let reason go.

But it was so nice to not have to pretend to be Someone Else for a moment.

And they say it's easier to talk to strangers than friends.

"What about you. What's your life like when you're not acting?"

I picked up some noodles and slurped them as he thought about his answer.

"I suppose it's the opposite. People don't see me, they confuse me with the characters I play."

"Ouch! Touché."

He exhaled a laugh as he picked up some noodles too, "It's an interesting change to be confused with a character before I play him."

I couldn't help laughing. "Is that why you go home? So the people you grew up with can remind you who you are?"

Oops, sprung! He'd know I'd Googled him now.

"Exactly so."

He caught my chopsticks in his. I'm not sure whether he meant to, but when I looked up at him, he was studying me intently.

My first thought was that I had soup on my face, so I wiped my lips with the back of my hand.

His eyes darted to my lips and back up again. I was looking at his lips as he reflexively licked them.

As helpless as a moth drawn to a flame, I couldn't stop myself leaning forward to kiss him. His soup flavoured lips were soft and warm.

As I started to pull away, he dropped his sticks and reached out with both hands to pull me back, kissing me deeply, passionately.

I was a little confused. I knew why I wanted him, well not Jason exactly, but I couldn't fathom what he wanted from me given we'd not spent more than about half an hour together.

That pesky reasoning part of me started up again, but I was committed to living this story now, if only for a short time, so I shut it down before it really got going.

He pulled away and looked at me closely.

Tentatively, he reached and undid one of my shirt buttons, and I wished I'd worn something with a lower neckline.

I think he was looking for some sign of rejection, and when it didn't come, he undid another button.

And then another, and smoothed his fingertips across my décolletage.

Which tingled so deliciously I gasped and shut my eyes.

It had been such a long time since a hand other than mine had been so intimate.

Did he feel the same sense of something missing?

His light touch was enough.

I dropped my chopsticks and went for his t-shirt, trying to get it over his head, but only succeeding in getting it caught on his ears.

He sort of shouldered me aside and stood to pull it off himself.

His hairless tanned chest was even more spectacular than I'd imagined.

I slowly reached up and gently placed my palm above his heart, and his muscles twitched.

As I looked up at him, he covered my hand with his and leaned down to kiss me again.

Ah yes, that was it.

I started tugging at my buttons and managed to get my shirt off.

I only avoided falling off the chair because he pulled me to my feet.

Still kissing me as he expertly undid my bra.

Oops, reason nearly got its foot in the door there.

Intoxicated once more by the scent of sandalwood, I ran my hands up his smooth chest and across the back of his shoulders holding him to my naked chest.

As he tried to straighten up, I wrapped my legs around his waist. He took a ragged breath and looked at me again.

"That way," I said waving a hand in the direction of the bedroom and gently bit his neck where the vein pulsed.

And at that point dear reader, we'll leave it there and imagine the swell of music, fireworks and waves crashing to the shore.

It was all that and more, but there are some things a girl has to treasure for herself and not dilute by sharing.

I hadn't expected Jason to still be there in the morning; Chang would've left during the night.

I was embarrassed, I didn't want Jason to know that I hadn't slept with him, and in the cold light of day, I wasn't sure that I wanted to have sex with him either.

Not to mention that I was a little hungover. And didn't want him to think I was just another fangirl.

My carry-on bag was already packed and waiting by the main suite door. I darted around the bedroom picking up my clothes, abandoning my toiletries and carefully tiptoeing out of the bedroom, quietly shutting the door behind me.

I dressed quickly, but not really quietly, and raced around the room collecting my laptop and handbag.

I was just about to exit stage right when I remembered I'd offered him a copy of the book.

I collapsed on a chair at the table for a moment, narrowly missing a bowl of cold soup, while I thought it through.

Should I just leave it?

Or should I write something in it?

Which name should I sign - true or pen?

Would he find it and take it, or would he leave it for the maid?

What would a Celebrity Author who'd had a one-night stand with the actor playing her hero do?

What would a woman who'd had the best sex in her sad, solitary life do?

I took the dog-eared copy I'd been using to refresh my memory with from my bag, shoved the half-eaten soup aside and using my trademark archival-quality purple ink pen (got to think of the fans) simply wrote

Thanks,

Amy

x

And then tiptoed back into the bedroom and left it on the bed next to him.

And exited quietly, stage left.

I had a plane to catch.

«« • »»

I thought of him many times over the next few months, and now and again I'd see him on the news with some pretty lady or other.

I didn't hear from him, so it seemed he was satisfied with the outcome of our night together.

In my more generous moments, I gave him the benefit of the doubt - he didn't know my true name.

But in less generous moments, I thought he might have at least tried. Others had found me with seemingly little difficulty.

But who was I kidding?

If I didn't know who I'd slept with, how could he? And it still wasn't clear why he'd slept with me.

Was he maybe doing his own research?

But there was no doubt our night together had inspired me.

I'd started writing almost before the plane had taken off, and General Chang's Egyptian Adventure was ready and waiting by the time my publisher asked for it.

How ironic that they'd waited so long to ask for a book to release at the same time as the movie.

At least they were prepared to rush it into print.

I'd written a charmingly cryptic dedication Jason would understand if he happened to see it.

And should he happen to read it, he'd probably recognise that I'd written what I knew.

Though I didn't know what he might think about that.

I hadn't heard a whisper about our brief interlude, or read any gossip about it.

While I was happy to avoid the speculation, I was still jealous of the pretty ladies.

I was surprised when my publisher called to let me know they were working together with the studio on a joint book and film promotion.

The studio would be making all the arrangements and would contact me in due course.

Book tours are always exhausting. Too much travel in too short a time, and too many people making too much noise.

It looked as though this would be a biggie - Jason's last movie had been a sell-out success, and he was now the hottest "new" star on the scene.

By the time my plane landed (in the middle of the night), I'd worked myself into a frenzy over what might happen.

With Jason, with the press, the movie, the book, the premiere.

I was so tense I thought I might snap!

I mentioned my vivid writer's imagination, right?

The horrors I'd imagined were nothing compared to what I walked into - cameras flashing, reporters calling out to me, people screaming.

It's not what I'm used to, and I thought the studio could have warned me.

I was very grateful the studio chauffeur was near enough to grab me and whisk me away in next to no time.

Though I suppose he was trained to wait just long enough for good exposure and no more.

I was also grateful I'd had the foresight to change my clothes, comb my hair and put on some lipstick before leaving border control.

Especially a couple of hours later when I saw my photo splashed across the morning papers.

JESSICA MASON AUTHOR OF
GENERAL CHANG MYSTERIES
ARRIVES FOR FILM PREMIERE.

I hadn't even had breakfast, and my book tour was off with a bang.

As was my studio assigned stylist.

I swear she did not stop talking the entire time she was measuring me, waving clothes at me to see what suited, and checking to see if I liked it.

She more or less kicked aside my poor travel bag as she hung my new studio approved wardrobe. Thankfully not too vampish, though perhaps slightly more librarian in style than my usual choices.

Howls of laugher - as if I'd chosen a style!

I'd be on morning TV within a couple of hours. So the stylist sent me to bathe and wash my hair while she ordered coffee and breakfast, and liaised with the hair and makeup artists.

When I came out, they rushed to style me and sent me back to the car with gift copies of the new Chang mystery (Jason's face prominently on the cover) for the hosts.

My assigned assistant gabbled at me about pitches and gifts for studio audiences and led me into a waiting room.

Which I paced up and down, summoning inner peace while waiting for my turn under the lights.

And then I was being hustled on set to explain where the stories came from. And how I felt about the film and what I thought about the Director and actors.

And off into the car for a change of clothes and a mid-morning show.

Then back to the car for a change of clothes and taping a spot for the evening news.

I didn't know it at the time, but there was a set of rooms like stables.

I sat in one, the Director in another, Jason and the female lead in a third, and some other people in yet other rooms. The reporters funnelled through, ten minutes with each of us to be edited to fit their needs.

He was right next door all along, and I had no idea. I'm amazed I couldn't feel his energy through the walls.

As my last reporter left and my gaggle of studio lackeys descended upon me through the open door, I caught sight of him walking down the corridor with his lackeys clamouring for his attention.

He gave me a tight smile as he strode past my door, neither pausing nor otherwise giving any indication of intimacy.

Just.

That.

Cold.

I couldn't tell if he was busy, discreet or just plain didn't care about me.

I felt myself slump as the scent of sandalwood in his wake hit me and dashed my unarticulated hopes.

But, I was there to do a job, so I squared my shoulders, straightened my spine and put on my Celebrity Author Persona.

I smiled at bookshop signings, performed readings, gracefully accepted the compliments of daytime TV, and laughed at inane Chang jokes.

Even Author events can be solitary and lonely events.

At the end of each day, I was so grateful to be back in the quiet stillness of my room that its empty storylessness didn't really bother me.

I ate room service and watched him on night time chat shows spruiking the movie.

He was charming, self-deprecating and amusing, relating stories about on set hijinks and praising the Director and his co-stars.

Not a word about me, though realistically, why would there be?

How does that Nat King Cole song go? Smiling, heart breaking, aching, whatever it is.

Naturally, the two clips they used were:

a. the climactic choreographed fight scene, and

b. the one where he steps out of the dark to swoop the damsel in distress up in his arms with a passionate kiss.

I could almost imagine his friends and family laughing at him and keeping his ego manageable.

How I wanted to be there with them rather than here in this celebrity merry-go-round.

The grim humour of being jealous of people I hadn't met was not lost on me.

How exactly had I come to this place of loneliness?

Damn you writer's imagination!

Finally, the night of the premier arrived, and I wasn't sure how I felt.

The clever studio stylist arrived before I had a chance to chicken out and refuse to go.

I hadn't forgotten my red-carpet story, and the stunning deep red bias-cut dress she offered was a powerful incentive.

It was elegant in its simplicity, with a demure high neckline, tight long sleeves and a full yet flat skirt.

We'll just gloss over how difficult it was to get into the foundation garments required for a smooth silhouette in a fitted dress. And how long it took to do up all the tiny pearl buttons down the back.

The hairstylist swept my hair up into a tall braided coronet.

Then it was time for makeup, again understated, and a spritz of some kind of madly sophisticated sexy musky fragrance.

Wicked Witch of the East ruby slippers, red clutch, diamond earrings, and an enormous diamond broach pinned to my left shoulder.

I was ready. Just in time for the chauffeur.

Now, I'm what they like to call petite.

In fact, I'm smaller than petite, but I felt as tall and glamorously beautiful as the best of them as I lifted my skirt Disney Princess style and started down the grand staircase.

How fortunate I'd taken some deportment classes for research and could descend stairs without looking at them.

I can't tell you how satisfied I was to find a throng of photographers waiting at the bottom.

I've no idea whether they were waiting for me, but I leaned nonchalantly on the bannister, posing prettily while I surreptitiously looked for my driver.

Nor can I say how surprised I was when Jason, still sporting Chang's hair and pencil moustache, appeared from the shadows.

He took my hand and brought it to his lips, then tucked it through his arm. "You look beautiful," he said.

"You're not too shabby yourself."

He looked gorgeous in a slim tuxedo, with his hair casually swept back from his face.

Unusually for a premiere, he wore a fresh red rose in his lapel. One that matched the colour of my dress exactly.

Clever studio stylist.

We stood for a moment before he bowed his head to the photographers and led me towards the exit.

Oh.

My.

God.

Not only was I a Princess for a few hours, but Jason Winter was my Prince Charming.

I'm so amazed I didn't trip or fall, my knees felt so weak!

Safely in the relative privacy of a dark windowed limousine, and enveloped in an intoxicating warm cloud of sandalwood, he kissed me.

Deeply.

Thoroughly.

Mintily.

I'm not sure about my lipstick, but when he was done, there was not one hair out of place on my head.

Which was swimming.

Do movie stars go to classes to learn how to kiss without messing up hair?

I'd have to look into that.

He cradled the back of my neck in his right hand, forcing me to meet his gaze, while gently caressing the edge of my chin with his thumb.

"I promise you, the next time we're together, you'll know you're sleeping with me, and not him."

And then he kissed me again.

My insides turned to jelly, and reason left me without a word to say in reply.

I wanted that so bad.

Right then and there would have been perfectly fine.

It seemed we arrived at the theatre in no time at all.

The chauffeur opened the door for Jason, who got out, then held out his hand to help me out of the car.

As I placed my hand in his, he bent to kiss it, and the photographers went nuts.

What was it with this guy and the hand kissing? Though, I kinda liked it.

My deportment lessons covered how to exit a car like a lady too, so all good there.

We stood, still holding hands as cameras flashed all around us. He looked down at me and smiled, which naturally made me smile back, and the photographers redoubled their efforts to get the perfect shot.

As the next car pulled in, he turned and led me up the stairs and into the dimly lit theatre.

Still holding my hand, which now trembled a little, he took me from group to group of actors and film industry people.

I *really* tried not to act like too much of a fangirl. And to be gracious when they said they loved my books.

Celebrity Author Persona had abandoned me, and in any case, it always makes me feel weird when someone compliments my work.

Soon enough, it was time to take a seat and watch the movie.

Movie Chang was edgier than mine; his movements more dynamic, and his attitude more aggressive.

I didn't really like this Chang, but there was no doubt he was magnetic.

Now and again I'd look over at the man whose fingers were entwined in mine.

As if sensing my confusion, he'd give me a small smile and squeeze my hand or smooth his thumb across the back of it.

And the audience would laugh, and I'd look up at him on the big screen again.

I mean I already knew he was not my Chang, let alone the hard man on the screen, but I didn't know who he was.

As screen Chang kissed Poor Girl and started taking her clothes off, I closed my eyes, so I didn't have to watch.

And as the light flickered through my closed lids, I wondered what his mother thought of his on-screen intimacies.

Yes, I was jealous - Poor Girl was doing a better job than I'd expected.

I wondered if his mother had met any of his co-stars.

And I wondered what she'd think of me.

All too soon the credits rolled, and the red velvet curtain closed.

The audience called for the Director who took to the stage and made a short speech praising the crew before calling Jason and his co-star on stage. They made their own speeches, but I wasn't listening.

My writing brain had kicked in, and I was thinking about a disaster at a movie premiere. How flammable were the furnishings, and what kind of fire retardant would they deploy and how long it would take to put the fire out.

I lost the plot when the sound of thunderous applause hit and a spotlight suddenly shone in my face.

"Ladies and Gentlemen," the Director announced, "I'd like to introduce you to the author of the General Chang books, Ms Jessica Mason. Please come on up Jessica."

I should have been paying attention.

Hopefully, he'd have explained what he wanted by the time I got up to the stage.

Fixing my eyes on Jason, I descended the stairs.

As I approached the stage, he came to meet me. Taking my hand, he bent to kiss my cheek and quietly asked, "Did you see enough of the movie to say something nice?"

I dipped my head in ascent and allowed him to escort me to the microphone.

I looked out over a sea of famous faces as the applause died down.

Turning to the audience on my right, I started with "Wow", and turning to the left, I shrugged my shoulder "I mean, just Wow."

Looking to the front, I fanned myself with an imaginary fan, "Ho boy, that was some movie."

A smattering of laughter.

I turned to smile at the Director, Poor Girl and Jason, "I think you've ruined the books for me."

The audience laughed, and applause broke out as I backed away from the microphone.

I'd planned to sidle behind the group, but Jason put his arm around my waist and pulled me back to stand between him and the Director as the photographers started up again.

No wonder he had to escape it all now and again.

It seemed to last forever, but I suppose it wasn't much more than a minute before the Director led us off the stage.

And along yet another red carpet for quick sound bite interviews, waving and autograph signing.

I prefer the solitary writing side of being an author, and Jason thwarted each of my attempts to skip ahead and away from the attention.

Whether he took my hand, clasped my waist or clutched my shoulder, there was no getting away from his touch.

The heat of his hands seared through my clothes, constantly reminding me of his promise.

Though I had no idea how he was going to get me out of the corsetry.

I was on fire, and I had no choice but to squirm discreetly and go with the flow.

Thank god the stylist had chosen something pretty as well as practical.

Finally, we made it to the end of the carpet and into a limousine heading to the after-party.

Alone, aside from the driver who discretely closed the connecting window.

Jason pulled me into his lap, and I became aware that I wasn't the only one who wanted to move things forward.

There wasn't much bare skin he could access, but he reached under the skirt and ran his hands up my legs to clasp my buttocks as he kissed me again.

Too soon the driver's tinny voice came over the intercom to say we were pulling into the hotel.

I slid off his lap and smoothed my skirt, trying not to smile as he adjusted his trousers.

And when the car door opened, I was ecstatic to find we were back at my hotel.

Sadly, no sneaking off just yet though, more photographers, and through to a big party of movie star peers to celebrate the end of the project.

Jason loosened his tie as he led me across to a love seat in a small alcove.

He sat and pulled me down next to him, one hand casually resting on my thigh as he toyed with my fingers with the other.

Clearing his throat, he looked at me, "I read your book."

"How nice. Which one?"

"The new one, the one you wrote for me."

I couldn't help myself, "did you buy it, or did the studio give it to you?"

He sighed, and I regretted the words immediately.

"I suppose I deserved that. I don't know where the book came from, I assumed you. Though now that I think about it, it was unsigned and came to my real name."

Ooh, you've got to love a good mystery, haven't you?

"I was angry when I woke and you'd gone. I couldn't believe you'd left me as if nothing had happened."

It was my turn to be ashamed. I opened my mouth to reply, but he pressed an index finger against my lips to stop me.

I resisted the temptation to lick it.

"You didn't seem to have any idea who I was, and we shared a strong attraction, so I thought we'd made a genuine connection. That despite what you said, you could see me through Chang and Jason. I don't know who I was more jealous of.

"And then I found this," he pulled aside his collar to reveal my every day chakra necklace."

So that's where it went.

"There hasn't been a day gone by that I haven't worn this and thought of you. I need to be with you, but I have no idea who you are."

I couldn't stand it any longer, I licked his finger.

His eyes darkened, and with a groan, he took my face in both hands and kissed me.

I thought I could get used to that.

"Can we go now?" I asked when he let me go.

And maybe we would, if the Producer hadn't arrived with champagne and a couple of guys from the crew.

Despite the timing, I was really glad to see them.

Blushing furiously, I patted Jason's leg and stood to talk to them. He stood too, and after a round of handshaking and congratulations, he said "I'll catch you later," and disappeared into the crowd.

I accepted some good-natured ribbing about Jason and followed the guys to chat with the rest of the crew.

Who introduced me to other people, and now and again, someone wanted to meet Jessica Mason.

Or the woman in red.

And all the while I was turning to see Jason looking back at me across the crowded room, though given my height that was nothing short of miraculous.

As the crowd started thinning out, he appeared behind me and snaked an arm around my waist.

It was time.

In an attempt to avoid detection, we left through a side door, skirted a utility area and took the service elevator.

Suddenly I was overcome with shyness and turned away from him.

"I thought of you too...

"I was afraid of what I might see in your eyes that morning. You're some hotshot movie star, and I'm just some daggy chick the studio flew in for the day.

"You probably have women throwing themselves at you every day - how can I compete with that?"

A tear rolled down my cheek as I took a ragged breath.

He kissed the nape of my neck, pulled me back against his chest and enclosed me in his arms.

"They don't see me like you do. I'm not even a person to them, something more like a scalp."

He dropped a kiss on the top of my head, then rested his chin on it. "We don't have to do anything you don't want to do. Now or ever."

Though a stray finger was idly drawing hot circles on my ribcage and it was almost more than I could bear.

Fortunately, the elevator binged to indicate our arrival at my floor.

I caught up my skirt in one hand, and grabbed his in the other and ran down the corridor.

I hoped that all those stylists had packed their bags and left.

And thank goodness they had.

Slamming the door behind us, ruby slippers on both feet, I leaned back against it and looked up at him.

He put his free hand on it for support and leaned down to kiss me, before crushing my body against his with the other.

I made a small sound, so he took my hand and led me to the bedroom where he started to unbutton the dress, dropping kisses down my spine as he went.

Every time I reached for him, he slapped my hand away.

Definitely not a Chang move.

Once the dress had fallen to the floor, I reached for him again, and he allowed me to do to the same for him while he pulled the pins from my hair and ran his fingers through it, smoothing it out across my shoulders.

Also not a Chang move.

And the next bit's private.

And the bit after that.

Then the next bit too.

Goodness me, let's just pick it up the next morning.

I lay on my side, one hand supporting my cheek and looked closely at him in the light.

He hadn't completely shaken Chang off; aside from the hair, there was still something dangerous about him.

I ran a finger lightly across the moustache and up his cheek to tuck his hair behind his ear, allowing my palm to cradle his cheek.

I wondered how long it took an actor to let a character go, or did the character become a part of them?

Did you just need to push the right button to bring them back to the surface?

Or was it like writing, where you left a piece of yourself behind forever?

He opened his eyes and looked at me for a moment before turning to kiss the palm of my hand.

"Coffee?" I asked.

He yawned and scrubbed his eyes, "Ah god, that would be wonderful."

I left him to make whatever morning preparations men need and set the espresso machine in motion.

Despite laying out two mugs, I forgot for a moment that he was there as I scratched my head, and combed my hair with my hands, dislodging a couple of hidden pins.

Eyes closed, standing on tip-toes I was stretching tall when his cool hands captured my breasts.

I'd forgotten I was naked too.

Laughing at my startled squeak, he offered me a robe.

We sat companionably drinking coffee, soaking up the warm sunshine on the balcony.

My feet rested in his lap, and he was idly stroking my leg under the robe.

It occurred to me that I still didn't know his true name.

"So, Mystery Man, if you're not General Chang or Jason Winter, what is your name?"

He took another sip of his coffee, and smiled enigmatically, "You tell me yours first."

Eyes rolled.

I held out my hand, "Amy Prescott."

He took it, turned it palm upwards and kissed it, "Hello Amy Prescott, my name is Song Kai. I'm very pleased to meet you."

"Kai." Oh, that was the perfect name.

"Kai, the pleasure is all mine."

THE END

ABOUT THE AUTHOR

Alexandria Blaelock writes stories, some of them for *Ellery Queen's Mystery Magazine* and *Pulphouse Fiction Magazine.*

She's also written four self-help books applying business techniques to personal matters like getting dressed, cleaning house, and feeding your friends.

She lives in a forest because she enjoys birdsong, the scent of gum leaves and the sun on her face. When not telecommuting to parallel universes from her Melbourne based imagination, she watches K-dramas, talks to animals, and drinks Campari. At the same time.

Discover more at www.alexandriablaelock.com.

9 781925 749489